Abstractedly, Mar **that they'd cleared** **they were out in the square with a handful of people milling around them.**

But she couldn't break the traction of Cayetano's stare. His heavenly masculine scent was in her nose. The powerful thud of his heartbeat danced beneath her fingers, his breathing a touch erratic again after his gaze dropped to linger on her mouth, his own lips parted to reveal a hint of even white teeth.

And just like that she was once again thrown to that night in Abruzzo when this foolish crush had taken a deeper hold. When the only thing she'd yearned for, more than anything else in existence, was to kiss Cayetano Figueroa. Who cared that she'd sworn to be rid of this madness a mere...half an hour ago?

Half an hour ago...while she'd been choosing the engagement ring he intended to give to another woman.

Her eyes started to widen. He sucked in a sharp breath.

A camera flash went off, dancing off the diamond ring she'd forgotten to take off and illuminating their expressions for a nanosecond before immortalizing it in life-altering pixels.

Accidentally Wearing the Argentinian's Ring

MAYA BLAKE

HARLEQUIN
PRESENTS

HARLEQUIN®
PRESENTS™

Recycling programs
for this product may
not exist in your area.

ISBN-13: 978-1-335-59347-4

Accidentally Wearing the Argentinian's Ring

Copyright © 2024 by Maya Blake

For questions and comments about the quality of this book,
please contact us at CustomerService@Harlequin.com.

TM and ® are trademarks of Harlequin Enterprises ULC.

Harlequin Enterprises ULC
22 Adelaide St. West, 41st Floor
Toronto, Ontario M5H 4E3, Canada
www.Harlequin.com

Printed in Lithuania

MIX
Paper | Supporting
responsible forestry
FSC® C021394

Maya Blake's hopes of becoming a writer were born when she picked up her first romance at thirteen. Little did she know her dream would come true! Does she still pinch herself every now and then to make sure it's not a dream? Yes, she does! Feel free to pinch her, too, via Twitter, Facebook or Goodreads! Happy reading!

Books by Maya Blake

Harlequin Presents

Reclaimed for His Royal Bed
The Greek's Forgotten Marriage
Pregnant and Stolen by the Tycoon
Snowbound with the Irresistible Sicilian

Brothers of the Desert

Their Desert Night of Scandal
His Pregnant Desert Queen

Ghana's Most Eligible Billionaires

Bound by Her Rival's Baby
A Vow to Claim His Hidden Son

Visit the Author Profile page
at Harlequin.com for more titles.

CHAPTER ONE

THERE WAS A reason Mareka Dixon's life was series of challenges centred around proving herself, whether it was beating the alarm clock and waking up before it went off, or getting off the bus two stops early to prove she could walk off that extra helping of ice-cream she'd had with dessert last night. Or proving she could kick herself six ways to Sunday when she thought about *him*.

She didn't need to be a psychologist to work out where it came from.

No—not now. There was an allotted time pocketed within her 'all work, zero play' life to contemplate her excess emotional baggage—Sunday nights between six and eight p.m., when she returned home after a visit to her parents.

Right now, she needed to concentrate on where she was going: Smythe Square, Knightsbridge.

Specifically, an establishment called Smythe's. Another one of those eye-wateringly chic and stratospherically expensive places where simply looking lost drew suspicious, disdainful glances, even from staff. Where her unfashionable corkscrew curls and curvy figure drew second and third looks, each one incrementally judgemental and condescending. Where sleek super-cars were as common as chips and prettily coiffed poodles wore accessories more expensive than her whole year's salary.

Today, she'd dressed for the fact that, as far as she was aware, her ultra-demanding, ultra-suave and astute billionaire boss was safely on the other side of the Atlantic. She hadn't bothered to spend a painstaking fifteen minutes to tame her wild hair, nor had she been as meticulous with her make-up as she usually was when he was in town. She'd made it in for seven-fifteen, however, and worked through her lunch as per usual, the demands from her two counterparts in New York and Argentina seemingly relentless.

But Mareka thrived on the challenge, because each week she remained Cayetano Figueroa's European PA was a notch on her CV that would be worth gold when it was time to move on.

And there would come a time because…

Nope, not thinking about that.

Mareka ignored the heat gathering in her belly and glanced at her phone. The blue map-dot said she was nearing her destination. She fingered the black card in her pocket for the dozenth time to make sure it was there. It had been the only thing nestled in the black box delivered to her office this afternoon by the sharply dressed courier, for the attention of Mr Figueroa.

As Cayetano's PA on this side of the Atlantic, Mareka was used to organising extravagant events and purchasing lavish gifts, the scale of which she'd only ever seen in over-the-top movies and TV shows. It had been a humbling and jaw-dropping experience to comprehend that, for men like her boss, spending like this was a run-of-the-mill activity.

Still, the cryptic delivery of the box and its contents were evidence that Mareka was operating on a whole new level. Which had made her doubly nervous when Cayetano had called an hour ago to inform her he was actually in London, at a meeting in Canary Wharf which had overrun.

Mareka hadn't wanted to examine why she felt disconcerted and hurt that her boss hadn't bothered to inform her he was in London. And, yes, it had been even more disquieting when the thought had triggered old feelings of inadequacy.

I don't need this...

She'd buried that feeling because, firstly, she needed to hang onto the best paid job she'd had in her life; and, secondly, because Cayetano Figueroa had been speaking at his usual fast clip, expecting her to follow and execute his every sexily accented word.

So, in her best crisp voice she'd answered. Yes, a box had arrived for him. Yes, it contained a black card with an address on the front, a phone number and what looked like a code on the back. Yes, she could most definitely visit the address in Knightsbridge and hold his place until he arrived.

Who cared that it was nearly seven p.m. and her only highlight on a Friday night was with her streaming service and a tub of her favourite ice-cream? So what if it was over twelve hours since she'd shoved her feet into three-inch heels, and the tight belt that cinched her Figueroa Industries-expensed designer suit was strangling her?

As of three months ago, she'd outlasted Cayetano's last four PAs. And, while her over-achieving parents would sneer at her, she would take that as a success, a vital steppingstone to achieving what *she* most desired. It was the reason she was risking exposing herself to feelings she shouldn't entertain towards her boss…

You have arrived at your destination.

Mareka jumped at the chirpy prompt from her phone, then froze on the pavement. Peering in through the glass frontage of the four-storey building, all she could see were striking paintings and pieces of art skilfully backlit to exhibition standards.

It was the sort of art her parents could spot and name at a thousand paces. The sort of art they'd expect her to utilise as fodder for 'skilful discord' on the rare occasions she was invited to one of their academia soirees. And it was the sort of painting that—when she inevitably failed their test and they snippily corrected her that, no, it was a Haydon, not a Margaux—she secretly vowed *never* to buy should she triumph over near-impossible odds and win the lottery.

'Excuse me, miss, are you lost?'

Mareka snapped into focus and blinked at the military-lean man watching her with naked suspicion from a dozen paces away.

'No, I'm exactly where I need to be, thanks,' she returned smartly.

Perhaps a little too smartly because, casting a quick glance around, Mareka could spot neither the name she sought nor an entrance to the art gallery.

Was *this* why she'd had to give up her evening in front of her TV—to pick up art for her boss?

Disgruntled, and a little terrified to make eye contact with the man whose crisp suit didn't disguise the tell-tale bulge of a weapon beneath his jacket, she reversed direction by several paces, only to be confronted with a carbon-copy guard.

'And where is that, exactly, miss?' the new guard demanded.

Despite the rush of traffic a few streets away, the square was ominously hushed, the growing scrutiny sweat-inducing.

'Because, if you have no business here, I suggest you leave before I'm forced to call the authorities,' Guard Number One snapped.

You're Cayetano Figueroa's representative—act like it.

Reaching into her pocket, she extracted the black card and held the small rectangle in front of her like a suit of armour. 'I have an appointment...' Mareka's words froze as both guards reacted, their transformation almost comical.

'Of course, madam. Apologies for the misunderstanding.' One arm swept out, deferentially ushering her up the short steps towards his colleague, who pivoted towards the wall next to him and swiftly tapped on a discreet panel. 'Please, this way.'

Mareka watched, goggle-eyed, as a twelve-foot door with no visible handle swung inward to reveal a wide, stunning hallway. The second guard stood to attention as she entered.

The click of her heels and the deeper footfalls of her escort echoed on the gold-veined cream marble. Several steps in and she realised that the magnificent foyer was in fact part of the art gallery, the artwork on display leading to a lift tucked in at the end of the space. A wide *chaise longue* sat beneath one giant painting she knew she recognised but couldn't quite place.

Mareka bit the inside of her lip as she looked around.

Did she wait? Take a seat and pretend to admire the art until Cayetano Figueroa arrived?

'The lift will take you to the floor you require, madam,' Guard Number Two said, his attitude much more cordial. 'You simply enter the code at the back of the card to activate it.'

Her nod was pure 'fake it till you make it', her insides knotting in bewilderment. Mareka willed her hands not to shake as she carefully inputted the numbers and watched the doors slide smoothly apart. The moment she stepped inside, the guard reached in, pressed the button for the second floor and promptly stepped back out.

'Have a good evening, madam.'

Since she wasn't sure she could speak, Mareka simply nodded, then sagged against the wall once the doors slid shut again.

As the lift surged up, so did her nerves.

If Cayetano hadn't sent her here to acquire a painting on his behalf, then why was she here?

The lift arrived far too quickly for her fraying nerves. Swallowing, she brushed her damp palms down her skirt and stepped out into a windowless space lit only with three exquisite and expensive-looking chandeliers. The walls were decked out in floor-to-ceiling rich, cream silk curtains with the same colours echoed in the plush grouping of sofas and luxurious carpet underneath her feet.

As with downstairs, there wasn't a single person in sight, but as Mareka approached the long banquet-like glass cabinet set out in the middle of the room, she got the faintest inkling why she was here. Because displayed beneath the spotless sheets of glass was row upon row of the most magnificent pieces of jewellery she'd ever seen in her life.

The first cabinet housed brooches in animal themes: a jet-black panther with eyes and curling tail made of diamonds; a hummingbird with feathers of sapphires, emeralds and rubies; a serpent formed entirely of yellow gold with scales of yellow diamonds.

The second cabinet held headdresses, crowns she'd only ever seen nestled on the heads of royalty in the pages of glossy magazines.

She was drifting, slack-jawed, towards the third cabinet displaying breath-taking necklaces and bracelets when a discreet, feminine cough sounded behind her. Mareka spun round to see a slim, tastefully dressed woman standing several feet away.

Dressed in a black boat-necked dress that cinched in at her narrow waist and flared to her knee, she was arresting in a way Mareka couldn't quite put her finger on. Perhaps it was the boxy glasses she wore, or the severely chopped sable-black hair Mareka was certain was a wig, that puzzled her. Or the bright-blue eyes instinct told her were contact lenses. She didn't have time to dwell as the woman stepped forward, her hand held out at a precise angle.

'Miss Smythe,' she stated in a voice completely devoid of inflection, as if she wanted to be forgettable.

As if...

Mareka took her hand, noting that the handshake was also entirely neutral, neither firm nor soft. 'Mareka Dixon.'

She glanced pointedly at the card Mareka held. 'I was expecting Mr Figueroa.'

'I...yes, I'm his PA. He's running a little late. He didn't want to miss his appointment and sent me in his place.'

A hint of displeasure flashed across her face but she

remained eerily composed. 'And will you be choosing the piece for him?'

Mareka's gaze darted back to the cabinet, her heart jumping into her throat. Deep down she knew the safest thing to do was to tell this mysterious woman that she preferred to wait for Cayetano. But...hadn't she'd lasted this long as the latest Figueroa PA because she listened to her instinct?

Feigning bravado, she nodded. 'Yes, I will.'

So what if her voice trembled a little when she glanced at the priceless pieces, and grew terrified at the thought of picking a piece for some unknown recipient without Cayetano Figueroa's express permission?

Faint amusement crossed the woman's face before it settled into staid neutrality once more. 'Very well. Come with me, please.' Skirting the cabinets, she aimed a device that looked like a miniature remote at the right wall.

As Mareka thanked her stars that she wouldn't be handling a diamond-festooned crown just yet, a pair of heavy silk curtains slid back to reveal another, smaller glass cabinet. Peculiar dread tickling her senses, Mareka was confronted with dozens of...engagement rings.

While shock unravelled through her like a waterfall, that wasn't the reason every cell in her body was reacting so negatively to the task she needed to perform. That could be attributed to a specific reason. The same reason every man who featured in her dreams sported moss-green eyes, wavy brown bronze-tinted hair and towered over six-foot-three. The same reason why they were sleekly built like the most streamlined of athletes, with mile-wide shoulders and lean hips.

Why they spoke with a distinct, pelvis-melting, Argentinian accent.

At some distinct, unforgettable point in the past year, while on a trip to the G7 Summit with her boss in Italy, she'd committed her most foolhardy act yet—an act that would probably damn her for ever in the eyes of her parents, if they found out. Not that she planned to divulge it to a single soul. She'd accepted a dinner invitation from her boss and finished dessert with a colossal crush on one of the most magnetic, intensely handsome and, according to the tabloids, most ruthless man on earth.

Did it matter that she'd immediately recognised the futility of her predicament and buried it deep? Judging by the distress churning within her as she stared at the white, velvet ring trays, not very much.

'Miss Dixon?'

Sucking in a breath, she raised her gaze from the display to the woman whose name suggested she was the proprietor of this ultra-exclusive establishment.

Even as the fierce urge to ask her *who* Cayetano was getting engaged to assailed Mareka, she dismissed it. She didn't need to add joblessness to her plight, and being indiscreet enough to demand to know who Cayetano intended to wed would most definitely risk just that. Snatching every crumb of composure she could find, she moved to the sofa and coffee table, which held a sterling-silver tray containing a bottle of vintage champagne set in an ice-bucket, two glasses and what looked like chocolate truffles.

Mareka had parcelled off enough of the same vintage to her boss's executive staff to know its worth. This wasn't a run-of-the-mill errand for her boss.

This was a life-altering event. A 'Cayetano Figueroa is getting off the 'world's most eligible bachelors list' type of event.

She cursed her knees for weakening as she sank onto the sofa, her dazed gaze fixed on the tray of rings. Which one would Cayetano grace his fiancée with? The rare blue diamond, perhaps? The pear-shaped pink diamond with the baguette side-stones?

Miss Smythe stepped forward, lifted the bottle and filled a glass with a quiet elegance that spoke of breeding. Whether it was cultivated or ingrained, Mareka was too distracted to tell as she accepted the chilled glass.

When the other woman murmured, 'I'll leave you to it,' all Mareka could manage was a nod, barely noticing her retreat.

She took a first sip of champagne, more to quiet the roiling within than anything else. If she was going to drown out the clamour of her foolish crush, what better way than with vintage champagne? She shook her head as hysterical laughter threatened, then jumped again as her phone buzzed. Setting down the glass, she hurriedly answered it.

'Miss Dixon, have you arrived?' Deep, unflappable, intensely masculine and utterly sexy in a way no other could sound; Mareka's belly flipped over at the sound of Cayetano Figueroa's voice.

Her shaking fingers tightened around her phone. 'Yes, I'm here.'

'*Muy bien.* I'll be there in half an hour. I'd prefer not to have to wade through a hundred samples. Have a small selection ready for me to inspect.'

'So…this is for you? You're getting engaged?' she blurted before she could hold her tongue.

Thick silence. '*Si.* I am.' The words were uttered in the same deep, unwavering timbre, which gave little indication as to his true feelings.

Something shrivelled up and died inside Mareka, and she hated it even more because it didn't set her free. Instead, the reflex that rose to her defence whenever her parents denigrated her surged to the fore. Holding on tight to it, she answered, 'Congratulations are in order, then, I guess.'

Another bout of silence dragged out—designed to make her squirm, or because of another facet to his character? Because why would Cayetano care about her feelings at all? Finally he responded with a rasped, *'Gracias.'*

'Would you like me to put together a press release? I could—'

'That will not be necessary. Everything is taken care of.'

That far too familiar pang of inadequacy lanced her. She breathed through it. 'Oh. Okay. I'll see you when you get here.'

'Indeed.' He rang off abruptly.

This is a good thing, she reassured herself as she reached for the champagne and gulped down another mouthful. If Cayetano was off the market, then she needn't expend any more of her day-dreaming on him! She needn't dwell on that 'moment' they'd shared at that dinner in Abruzzo, when she'd been one hundred percent sure her boss had wanted to kiss her.

She could devote her evenings and weekends to more productive endeavours. Such as taking the first step towards her lifelong dream of creating a charity to help younger women advocate for themselves. She'd saved enough to get a small foundation going, hadn't she?

She attempted to close her mind to the voice that whispered that it wasn't enough. That *she* would never be enough…

And what if she failed?

Heart squeezing, she pushed the line of doubts aside and forced herself to look at the sparkling gems. With another sip of champagne to bolster her, she plucked the first ring from its setting, gasping as the light caught and danced off the exquisite oval diamond.

Setting it to one side, she picked up another, then another. On the sixth, she paused, her breath catching at the flawless, cushion-cut diamond surrounded by pink micro-pave stones. It was beautiful, feminine and so utterly gorgeous.

She wasn't going to try it on. *No. No way.* That way lay madness. Setting it down, reluctantly, she grabbed the bottle and refilled her glass. Fifteen minutes later, she'd selected eight rings, each stone perfect enough to make any woman swoon. Especially with a man like Cayetano Figueroa going down on one knee, his heart-throbbing, chiselled face tilted up as he…

No—enough. That way most definitely lies madness.

Her gaze returned to the dazzling rings—specifically, the cushion-cut diamond. *It was so beautiful.* Surely it wouldn't do any harm if she slipped it on for one moment?

The giddiness in her belly screamed *yes*. She would most likely never return to a place like this: this moment in time was a fluke. Why not see how the other half lived?

Before she could talk herself out of it, she set down the glass with an unsteady click, a shocked, impish giggle escaping her as she reached for the ring… A fantasy of one Argentinian man sliding it onto her finger and completing the beautiful illusion with that kiss they'd never shared swelled like the best forbidden fairy tale.

Mareka's mouth gaped in wonder. Turning her hand this way and that under the chandelier, she gasped as the stones caught fire and shone. 'Oh! How utterly gorgeous you are!' Conscious that she was talking to an inanimate object while being slightly tipsy, she giggled again, lifting her hand for a closer look. 'I don't care,' she murmured. 'You're worth every moment of temporary madness.'

She yelped at the deep throat-clearing, rushing to her feet in panic. She knew who it belonged to; she didn't want to face it, even though the force of his presence rushed at her, taking hold and commanding the attention he believed was his due.

It took a moment of Mareka cringing in dismay before she lowered her hand and faced the statue-still form of Cayetano Figueroa standing not more than three feet away. She met those intense moss-green eyes boring into her like industrial-sized drills. His hands might have been shoved into his pockets, his bespoke jacket open and his tie loosened the way he tended to wear it after a crushingly long day, but Mareka wasn't fooled for a moment by his easy stance.

She stumbled back because everything Cayetano felt was displayed in his eyes: irritation; disbelief; thick cynicism. Maybe a hint of pity…?

It was that last emotion that stayed and seared. It reflected what she'd seen far too frequently in her parents' eyes. But it was a hundred times more potent in this man's eyes—enough to make her take another desperate step back, gasping in alarm as she caught her heel in the carpet. Her arms windmilled and she knew without a shadow of a doubt that she was about to pitch over like a sack of potatoes.

As shame filled her bloodstream and air rushed into her ears, she closed her eyes, unable to watch another demeaning expression flit across his face. So she didn't actually see him lunge forward, hands whipping out to catch her, one arm banding her waist, the other cupping her shoulder.

But, oh, did she feel him as he pulled her close, his powerful athletic body plastering hers from chest to thigh.

'Are you all right?' he murmured in her ear, his breath brushing her earlobe and sending a delicious shiver cascading over her.

She opened her eyes. Perhaps it was a combination of where they were, the rarefied air of the jewellery establishment, the idealistic fantasy she'd indulged in minutes ago or just the sheer magnetic, animal attraction she'd felt toward her boss for so long that made her reach for him too, her hand curling over his shoulder and brushing the hair at his nape.

'Yes.' She breathed. 'I… I'm fine.'

He continued to hold her, to stare down at her, as if doubting her response. Her blood thickened, her breath fluttering wildly as she waited and watched his gaze drop to her mouth, his own breathing sharpening. Sweet heaven, was he about to…?

The ear-piercing shriek that ripped through the room sent her jumping a mile high, her already racing heart thundering harder as she attempted to find the source.

Cayetano jerked them both upright, his eyebrows clamping in a frown as his gaze sharpened from volcanic heat to edgy wariness.

'Is that what I think it is?' he demanded, barely needing to raise his voice to be heard.

The mysterious owner nodded, magically reappearing. 'I'm afraid so. We must evacuate the building. Please come with me.' Without waiting for them, she turned on her heel.

Cayetano glanced down at Mareka, a pinched look setting his features as he released her and stepped back. 'After you, Miss Dixon.'

Mareka took a step, then felt her foot give way. She cringed. Oh God, she *really* shouldn't have had that second glass of champagne, especially on an empty stomach.

Hyper-aware of Cayetano's presence behind her, she tried to quicken her steps, following Miss Smythe's swaying figure to a landing and steps that led down. Reaching for the handrail, Mareka took one step down, then stumbled again.

Behind her, Cayetano uttered a muted curse, then strong hands were sweeping her off her feet. 'W-what are you doing?' she stammered as she was tucked against a hard-packed chest.

'Preventing us both from being burnt to a crisp, ideally.'

Mareka squeezed her eyes shut for a moment, growing intensely aware of his arm beneath her thighs and around her back, of the rippling muscle of flesh beneath the hand she braced against his torso. 'I can walk, you know,' she protested feebly.

'Evidently not efficiently enough in those heels. And most definitely not in an emergency,' he rasped, the rumble of his voice seductively moving through her.

Mareka's face heated and she admonished herself for the trailing pang that reminded her yet again that she was useless. That her inadequacies were always lurking, ready to shame her. 'Well, if you'd waited one more second instead of swooping in like a caped superhero, you'd have seen me take off my heels so I could take the stairs a little quicker.'

In the dim stairwell, his eyes glinted at her even as he

took the stairs with an assuredness that bordered on arrogant. 'I'm a little short on time today, Miss Dixon. Feel free to get your next saviour to enact that scene for you,' he stated dryly.

Her fingers dug into his shirt as he sped up, his feet making light of the stairs. Mareka couldn't quite curb the snort that erupted from her throat. 'Yeah, right. As if I'm ever going to be in this position again.'

The words emerged way more mournfully than she'd intended. Her face heated further, her gaze locked on his hooded expression as her words bounced between them. Scrambling for something that would dissipate the atmosphere, and finding nothing but turbulent thoughts better kept to herself, Mareka let out a stupid little whimper. Because now her boss was staring at her as if she were a specimen beneath his microscope, all her emotions on display for him to explore.

Abstractedly, she registered that they'd cleared the building and were out in the square with a handful of people milling around them. But she couldn't break the traction of Cayetano's stare. His heavenly masculine scent was in her nose. The powerful thud of his heartbeat danced beneath her fingers, his breathing a touch erratic after his gaze dropped to linger on her mouth, his own lips parted to reveal a hint of even white teeth.

And, just like that, she was once again thrown back to that night in Abruzzo when this foolish crush had taken a deeper hold. When the only thing she'd yearned for was to kiss Cayetano Figueroa and find out if the flashes of hot, Latin magnificence she'd imagined lived up to her fantasies. Who cared that she'd sworn to be rid of this madness a mere…half hour ago?

Half an hour ago…while she'd been choosing the engagement ring he intended to give to another woman.

Her eyes started to widen. He sucked in a sharp breath. A camera flash went off, dancing off the diamond ring she'd forgotten to take off and illuminating their expressions for a nano-second before immortalising them in life-altering pixels.

CHAPTER TWO

OF COURSE THINGS would happen this way.

Hadn't he been lurching from one crisis to another for the last three months? His mother had checked herself into a secret rehab, probably another ploy to torture his father and to bring unwanted attention to Cayetano.

His latest deal hovered on a knife's edge.

His fake fiancée was refusing to sign the pre-nup she'd agreed to a month ago.

Now his tipsy London PA—deep down, the reason he knew he chose to conduct his European business remotely as often as possible; the reason he'd *almost* crossed a strict professional line one night in Italy—had just landed them on the front page of the tabloids, her with a ring on her finger.

Cayetano swung towards where the flash had come from, despite knowing it was futile to confront the culprit. By now the picture would be in a greedy tabloid hack's inbox or splashed across social media. He bit back the growl that threatened to explode from his throat. The hand braced against his chest curled, fisting his shirt as she wriggled in his arms.

He redirected his focus back to Mareka, his senses sparking with what he wanted to think was irritation. *Dios*

MAYA BLAKE   25

mio, he'd almost kissed her back there. If she hadn't distracted him with that absurd conversation about superheroes in capes, he would've been more alert. He wouldn't have relished her delicious weight in his arms, marvelled at how soft and firm her skin was or wondered how her lips would taste beneath his.

This was her fault.

She gasped, then those delectable lips pursed in outrage. 'Excuse me?'

He realised he'd spoken his accusation out loud as footsteps approached. His bodyguards arrived at the same time as he set her down, unable to take his eyes off her face as she glared up at him.

'What do you mean, it was my fault?'

He glanced pointedly at the hand still braced on his chest, the diamond ring on full display for all to see. At least she had the grace to redden at his speaking look.

'I employ you for your discretion, Miss Dixon. This is far from discreet.' He breathed, mindful of their growing audience.

She opened her mouth to speak, but his bodyguard interjected, '*Perdón*, Señor Figueroa. We came as fast as we could.'

Cayetano was irritated by how hard it was to drag his eyes from Mareka to give a brisk nod. He could hardly blame them for the fire alarm going off. What he could do was direct his ire towards the woman who stared at him with a mixture of nervousness and defiance, then lowered her hand from his chest and curled it into a fist to hide the evidence of the ring.

His lips pursed. 'It's far too late for that now.'

'It's not my fault. The fire alarm went off. I tried to

say something, but you were too busy sweeping me off my feet.'

Her blush deepened as she spoke, and for an absurd reason Cayetano found himself staring at her mouth again. Her very lush, very pink mouth.

He cursed the heat weaving through him. This was *not* the time for this. And most definitely not with this woman.

His jaw clenched tighter as he remembered the other woman who was contributing to the other crisis in his life. There was a reason he kept his life free of emotional entanglements.

'Bring the car around. We're leaving,' he instructed his bodyguards. 'And you're coming with me, Miss Dixon.'

'But I thought...'

He raised his eyebrow. 'You thought?'

Her delicate, pointed chin rose. 'I have plans this evening.'

He told himself the reason he objected was because he didn't want to be inconvenienced. His day had been hellish from the start. 'Cancel them.'

Rebellion blazed in her eyes. 'Why should I?'

He allowed himself a tight smile. 'Because, according to a document lodged on a hard drive in my HR department, when I'm in town you will be available to me twenty-four hours a day. In return, you get to keep your own hours when I'm not. A contract you signed of your own free will. Am I mistaken?'

His voice was cool...reasonable, even, Cayetano assessed. And yet he felt almost volatile, staring down at her. Had he ever noticed this strain of defiance before? Was it a product of something else, like that almost-kiss? She wouldn't be the first PA who had committed the grave misfortune of developing feelings for him. Hell, it was why he'd got rid of her three predecessors.

But Mareka, that aberrant night in Abruzzo notwithstanding, had surprised him in the last eighteen months by being efficient without being intrusive.

Had he been wrong? Did he have another crisis on his hands?

'Well, you're not wrong, but I wasn't expecting you—'

'I wasn't aware I had to send you my diary to get you to fit me in, Miss Dixon.'

Her face tightened a fraction, drawing his attention to the smoothness of her jaw, the slender line of her neck. 'You don't need to put it like that, sir.'

Aware of the sparks still fizzing inside him, he took a step closer. 'I'd rather you not compound your gross error of judgement with insubordination. Would you?'

She glanced from his face to the car that was pulling up beside them. Then she shook her head. 'No.'

'That is the first sensible answer you've provided this evening.' He nudged her towards the vehicle. 'Get in.'

She took one step towards his car and wobbled on her feet again. A different sort of sensation churned in his stomach. He'd seen the half-finished bottle of champagne on the table upstairs. Now, peering down at her, he wondered whether it was just a blush that stained her cheek, or an alcohol-induced flush. Cayetano wasn't sure exactly why he felt so strongly about it.

Yes, you are.

He suppressed the emotion and forced himself to relax. But when she took another step, and immediately twisted on her heel, he couldn't quite bite back the growl. 'You are testing my patience, Miss Dixon.'

'I'm sorry to hear that, but the fire alarm has stopped. Are you sure you don't want to return upstairs?'

His lips formed one small, tight smile. 'Considering our very public exit, and the fact that we've already been photographed, I sincerely doubt we would be allowed back.'

Her eyes widened. 'Really? Why not?'

'Because Miss Smythe values extreme discretion above all else. Gaining re-entry might be permitted, but I'm certain it won't happen tonight.'

She looked over her shoulder, as if to make sure he was telling the truth. His nostrils flared as he tried to gather his patience. But as he inhaled his PA's unique scent assailed him, as it had done on the way down the stairs. A mixture of crushed flowers, it lingered far too alluringly.

'Get in,' he ordered again.

Perhaps she sensed his fraying temper because she obeyed without further argument. But the moment she secured her seatbelt, the action dissecting her ample breasts, she began to tug off the diamond ring as if it offended her—the same ring she'd so longingly admired upstairs.

'Here, I believe this is yours.'

He held up his hand. 'It stays on your finger for now.'

Her jaw sagged and her eyes clouded with confusion. 'What? But don't you need to return it? Or give it to your fiancée, whoever she is?'

Fastening his own seatbelt, his mood soured at the thought of Octavia and the drama she was creating back in Argentina. And as they drove away from the square he stared at the ring, now lying in Mareka's outstretched palm, begrudgingly accepting that it was the same one he would've chosen. But it wasn't Octavia's style. It wasn't ostentatious enough.

'Mr. Figueroa?' Her voice was firm but a little hesitant.

'How much champagne did you have to drink?' he asked abruptly, the issue bothering him more than he was willing to examine.

'What?'

'You heard me.'

She reared back in offence, but her long lashes swept down, her lips firming a little. 'It wasn't much. And I haven't eaten since breakfast. Maybe the second glass wasn't entirely advisable but it's not fair to blame me for any of the chaos back there.'

Perhaps he wasn't being fair, but his hellish few weeks didn't make him feel charitable. 'You don't think so? I can come up with at least half a dozen ways it could've gone.'

'Do you want me to apologise? Fine—I'm sorry.'

The sliver of intent that sparked through him surprised him at first, but as it thickened and grew Cayetano relaxed against his seat.

'You'll have a chance to redeem yourself yet. As soon as we get an idea of just how bad things are.'

Cayetano found out much too soon.

The buzzing in his pocket as he entered his hotel signalled that yet another crisis awaited him. From the looks directed his way as he strode across the open space, he knew the picture had already found several homes on the Internet.

Stifling a curse, he shortened his footsteps, aware that the woman who'd caused all of it was scurrying along behind him. He turned towards his harried looking PA. Beneath the chandelier of the five-star hotel that was his home when he stayed in England, the light glinted off her dark-golden locks, sparking another uncharacteristic thought.

'Your hair is different.'

Her eyes flared again, her hand darting up to the shoulder length. 'Yes, I wear it naturally sometimes.'

'You mean it's not usually straight?' He wondered why the question drew another flare of heat as she shook her head.

'No, it's not.'

He bit back the urge to instruct her never to straighten it again. What the hell was wrong with him? Was it a side effect of the relentless upheavals he'd faced in the last three months? His parents' marriage was forever on the brink of collapse, cynically held together only by financial incentives, and he was caught perpetually between the two.

He'd thought himself immune to his role but lately, with his mother's alcohol-fuelled emotions becoming increasingly erratic, Cayetano had found himself more on edge in his already strained relationship with his parents. *That* was yet another drama waiting for him back in Buenos Aires.

He stabbed a finger at the lift button. Entering his code, he held the doors for his PA, who hesitated, watching him with a wariness that set his teeth on edge. The moment they were alone, he addressed the issue chafing at him. 'Let's get a few things straight, shall we? How much do you drink on a daily basis?'

'How dare you? You have no right to ask me that.'

He took a deep breath and shoved his hands in his pockets. It was either that or frame that far too delicate jaw and run his hands over her heated cheek. A move that would most likely earn him a ticket to an employment tribunal.

'Since you were operating under my instructions, I think I'm well within my rights, don't you?'

'I told you already—I don't normally drink, and I had the champagne on an empty stomach.'

He stared down at her, attempting to see beneath her bluster. Her fire was pure enough for Cayetano to give her the benefit of the doubt. 'Very well. I believe you.'

Her shoulders sagged a little and she swallowed. 'Thanks,' she said, a touch snippily, and perhaps what he deserved.

He wasn't sure why that sent a flicker of amusement through him. The situation was far from humorous. He'd seen far too often what alcohol did to his mother.

As if on cue, his phone buzzed again as he entered his penthouse. Ignoring it, he crossed the living room to the phone sitting on the coffee table. Lifting it, he placed an order and hung up. Then he poured a tall glass of water from a crystal carafe. Approaching Mareka, where she lingered by the arch between the hallway and the living room, he held it out.

'Drink this. Dinner will be delivered in fifteen minutes. I have a few phone calls to make. Then we need to talk.'

She tried to hide the flare of alarm in her eyes. 'Talk about what?'

He paused on his way to his study. 'I suspect the next fifteen minutes will be crucial, Miss Dixon. Just pray that the outcome is more congenial for you than I expect it will be.'

Mareka opened her mouth to ask him what he was talking about, but Cayetano was walking away, his purposeful strides expressing firmly that he didn't intend to explain himself.

Her hand shook, sloshing water all over her wrist and

onto the marble floor. Grimacing, she gulped down a few mouthfuls. If she'd refused the champagne earlier, she wouldn't be here.

But she hadn't done anything wrong! Had she? She hadn't even asked to be saved from a potentially dangerous situation. She bit her lip, hating the spike of guilt declaring her ingratitude.

Striding into the lavish living room of the penthouse in the Hainesborough Hotel, she hesitantly unfurled the tight fist she'd wrapped around the diamond ring.

After seeing the other jaw-dropping pieces on display, Mareka knew without a doubt that the ring in her hand was worth a substantial fortune. And yet Cayetano had treated it like it was a cheap trinket. Hell, both he and the mysterious Miss Smythe hadn't even bothered to secure it when the alarm had gone off. Mareka wanted to think it was because her boss trusted her, or that the jeweller had an agreement with her rich clients, enough not to bat an eyelid when they swanned off with a ring worth a king's ransom.

But Mareka couldn't help the bitterness that surged through her belly. The kind of money people like Cayetano played with and discarded could change lives. The kind of change that could either mean a life led with dignity or burdened by self-doubt and drudgery. The kind of change *she* had sworn to use her charity to bring about. The more she stared at the ring, the more she wanted to be rid of it.

Whirling away from the window, she wandered down the same hallway Cayetano had taken. As she neared the open doorway, his thick curse, muttered in his mother tongue, slowed her feet.

'How foolish of me to think I had even ten minutes

to get this under control.' The words were set with such heavy sardonicism that Mareka flinched. 'So, what does she want now?'

She held her breath, knowing she shouldn't be eavesdropping, but unable to move. A handful of seconds later, Cayetano burst into laughter. Except there was nothing amusing about the sound ricocheting around the space.

'Are you serious?' Whatever response he received drew another curse. Then, 'No. You will do no such thing. I'll speak to her myself.'

The digital beep of the call ending drew another wince from Mareka.

Move.

Her feet refused to obey. She stood there, the priceless ring clutched tight in her fist, as Cayetano placed another call.

'Octavia…' He breathed.

Mareka's heart jumped into her throat. Octavia Moreno was Cayetano's Argentinian PA. The pictures she'd seen of the stunning woman was enough to ruffle any woman's confidence. Even from this side of the door, Mareka could hear the heated, sultry tones of the PA who'd worked for Cayetano for over six years.

'I hear you're still refusing to sign the pre-nup,' Cayetano drawled, an edge of irritation in his tone. Whatever answer she gave made him exhale. 'That is not what we agreed before I left Buenos Aires.' A pause. 'Of course I value you. But I also need to be able to take you at your word when—' He stopped as a torrent of Spanish spilled out of the phone.

Mareka's eyes widened at the borderline-shrewish outburst.

Before today, Mareka would've sworn that no one

would dare to speak to her formidable boss that way, and yet the evidence was unquestionable. From her own strict, albeit occasionally charged, relationship with Cayetano Figueroa, she would've sworn that he would never dally with an employee—that the rumours he'd once dated Octavia Morena were simply malicious lies.

Listening to the heated exchange now, Mareka reversed that assumption. Was this a quarrel between lovers?

Her stomach churned, threatening mild nausea at the thought. Her hand rose to her mouth as if she could stop the bile rising into her throat just by willing it away.

She *really* shouldn't have drunk that champagne. And, with the mood her boss was in, she doubted she was doing herself any favours by eavesdropping. Forget lasting six years—she might not make it another six *minutes*!

And what had he meant by 'the next fifteen minutes'? The question scythed through her hazy brain, sending her scrambling to retrieve her phone from her bag.

Cayetano could only have meant one thing—*the picture of them outside, in Smythe Square.*

'We're getting nowhere with this, Octavia, and you should know better than to threaten me with a deadline.' He inhaled sharply at the muffled response Mareka couldn't hear over her thundering heartbeat.

'*Basta.* I have another call coming through. I'll call you back shortly. I suggest you take the time to think things through properly.'

The doorbell rang.

Hurrying to the door before she was caught eavesdropping, Mareka opened it to the executive chef, who introduced himself as Manzano and wheeled in his silver trolley with a familiarity that said he'd done this many times. Feeling a little unnerved by the whole evening,

Mareka followed him into another jaw-dropping space that boasted floor-to-ceiling views of London.

She kept out of the way as the chef unpacked the heavenly smelling dishes onto the smoked-glass dining table, set out the cutlery and, with a courteous nod, took his leave.

Silence interspersed with bursts of furious Spanish kept her rooted in place for several minutes. Then the combination of the incredible aromas and her belly's increasingly growling demands sent her to the table. Grilled lobster and roasted vegetable on the first platter made her groan. Plates of what were discreetly labelled on the silver dish as 'Argentinian steak with buttered asparagus' made her mouth shamelessly water. Another six dishes she was sure could easily feature in a high-end gourmet's magazine severely weakened her resistance.

Quickly sliding the diamond ring back onto her finger before—*horror of horrors*—she misplaced it, she pulled out a chair and sat down, reminding herself that Cayetano had told her to eat…because they needed to talk when dinner was over.

She considered serving a plate for him. The volley of ferocious chastisement echoing down the hall suggested she was better off staying put.

Mareka had just finished sampling a tiny portion of every dish—ignoring the expensive bottle of wine breathing in the middle of the table, and opting for more water until she was sure her light intoxication had passed—when Cayetano strolled in.

She most definitely wasn't going to watch him walk towards her with that prowling gait that made her think of graceful predators, of kings of the jungle. She wasn't going to stare at that breath-taking face evocative of stunning works of art that graced museums. She most definitely wasn't going to glance at those mouth-watering lips and wonder what would've happened in that jewellery house, had she given into the madness and kissed him when he'd stared at her lips.

No. No. No.

Not looking didn't mean she couldn't *feel* the volts of energy vibrating off him or couldn't sense that something had him positively seething.

Something, she suspected strongly as he drew closer, that involved *her.*

The next fifteen minutes…

Four words that made her discard the vital need to avoid him, her gaze scrambling to meet his and see pinched lips and pure displeasure bouncing off his mile-wide shoulder.

A combination that made her clear her throat while scrambling to stand. 'Is…is everything okay?'

'No, Miss Dixon. Everything is most definitely not okay,' he replied in a voice coated in fire and ice as he rounded the table towards her.

Livid green eyes pierced hers. Then he set his phone down, face-up, and shoved it towards her.

She held his gaze a few more seconds, primarily because she couldn't drag her eyes from the hypnotic power and vortex of his, but also, because she was a little terrified to glance at his phone.

Curiosity won out. Her gaze dropped. A gasp flew unbidden from deep inside her. His low, animalistic growl echoed the turbulent sensation spinning around them.

'I see you concur—that this is much worse than I thought.'

'I… It's… How could…?' She stopped, judging it was

wise to shut up than attempt in any way to ascribe an explanation to the vivid picture on his screen.

But, really, what could be worse than this? What could land her in further disaster than seeing the way her hand was pressed deep into Cayetano Figueroa's shirt, her face tilted up to his, his angled down at hers? And, worst of all, the priceless diamond blatantly blazing on her finger...

The headline screamed: *Figueroa's Secret Love Revealed!*

As she stared in cringing stupefaction, he calmly flicked to another, even worse, headline.

Figueroa Proves Office Romances Are Still Alive and Kicking!

Out of the Boardroom... Headed Down the Aisle!

'Okay, that's enough.' Her plea was hoarse, barely intelligible.

He swiped his phone off the table, his precise movements belying the flames alive in his eyes.

She scrambled to quench the fire. 'Look, before you go blaming me again, I've already told you I didn't mean for any of this to—'

'The way you keep protesting makes me think the opposite.'

'What? No, you're wrong!'

'Am I?' he challenged silkily. 'There's no shame in admitting it. You wouldn't be the first to spot an opportunity and capitalise on—'

'I would take great care before you finish that sentence if I were you!' she protested hotly.

'Oh yes? And why is that?'

'Because you couldn't be more wrong if you tried,' she shot back, aware her breathing was erratic and her palms tingled. Dear God, it was almost as if she wanted to slap his drop-dead gorgeous face. She, who'd never entertained bodily harming another person in her life!

Perhaps he sensed the volatility that infected the room. For an age he simply stared, his gaze delving deeper with each passing second. Then a muscle rippled through his jaw. 'We are where we are, Miss Dixon. I'm more interested in where we go from here,' he said with chilling finality.

Her heart ricocheted behind her ribs. 'Well, the obvious response is to tell the truth. I can have a press release drafted in five minutes that this was all a huge misunderstanding.' Nervous laughter spilled out as she shook her head. 'I don't even know why the tabloids are in such a frenzy. Surely they know that you…and I…? That this will never be a possibility…?'

Her voice trailed off, her mouth drying as something untamed flared in his eyes. He was so at variance with the boss she knew that she wondered if he was suffering from some unknown condition.

Scratch that—maybe she needed to worry about her own condition. Because, when that scorching gaze left her face to chart a path over her body, lingering with that same penetrative demand, she feared she would never again be able to take a full breath.

'Enlighten me why you think not, Miss Dixon,' he invited with a voice so soft and deadly, it sent seismic tremors charging over her.

'B-because I'm your employee, for starters,' she blurted a little desperately. A totally disingenuous protest, because the thoughts she'd had about this man for the better part of a year had crossed the professionalism line a long time ago. Her face heating at the reminder, she ploughed on, boldly doubling down on the excuses she'd told herself in the dark. 'And because you…you're not my type either.'

She didn't dwell on what his response might be to her declaration, but the last thing Mareka had expected was for him to blink those silky eyelashes that were unfairly wasted on a man, before his shoulders shook in distinct amusement.

Her mouth dropped open in wonder. In all her time working for him, she'd never seen Cayetano Figueroa smile, never mind laugh. That it was entirely at her expense didn't even seem significant in that moment. Not when she couldn't drag her gaze from the sensual curve of those lips as they twitched. Nor stop herself from yearning to see what true mirth, full and unfettered, would look like on him. If this was a hint, he would be simply breath-taking.

'Are you sure? I recall an after-summit dinner a year ago when you all but *melted* in my arms,' he drawled wickedly.

No.

By mutual unspoken agreement, they'd never mentioned that incident. It had been her first and only G7 Summit with her new boss, the invitation to attend alone having ramped up Mareka's excitement. Hell, it had been one of the very few occasions she'd caught a glimpse of something approaching respect in their eyes when she'd told her parents.

High on a shocking number of successful deals for his company, Cayetano had taken her to a Michelin-starred restaurant—another first. And somewhere between dinner and the walk back to their hotel she'd found herself in Cayetano's arms under a starlit night sky. His lips had hovered dangerously, *roguishly* close, his strong, muscled arms holding her, drawing a lustful sigh from her. She'd felt the magnificent power between his legs, her own secret place responding with shockingly wanton arousal. His thick groan and incoherent Spanish words had drawn delicious shivers, the anticipation of his kiss *finally*, after months of secret yearning, making them strain closer.

In her lowest moments, Mareka cursed the police siren that made Cayetano stiffen, his eyes flaring in alarm before, cursing, he'd quickly released her. He hadn't explained or apologised. Neither had she. They'd swept the incident under the carpet.

But it had never gone away. Definitely not for her, since she'd revisited it with shameful regularity for months after it had happened.

'I suppose you're about to blame me for that too?' she asked shakily, the power of recollection, of awakening arousal, hammering through her.

A look passed through his eyes.

'Not for that, no. We were trapped in a…moment.' His voice was pure, sinful silk. 'But it proved my point then, as it does now—that I'm yours and *every* heterosexual woman's type.'

Mareka wanted to weep with how utterly right he was. She was battling with the injustice of all it all, scrambling for a rapier-sharp retort to the arrogance-soaked works, which was why she almost…almost missed the conclusion to his conceited statement.

'Which is why not a single person will dare to question us when we capitalise on this unfortunate but possibly significant opportunity.'

It was her turn to blink, although she doubted she looked half as sexy doing so. Time to try and force her brain to connect the vital dots. And, when she couldn't, to inhale and ask, 'I'm sorry, opportunity for what, exactly?'

'For you to fix what you've broken. Because, you see, with those images now splashed across every digital medium, I find myself regretfully minus a fiancée.' Another ripple went through his jaw. 'So I have no option but to pivot to the alternative. And that alternative, Miss Dixon, is you.'

Pivot… Alternative… Surplus… *Dispensable*…

Mareka ignored the hurtful bruising occurring inside her and reached for the anger triggered by his repugnant words. 'Excuse me? Where the hell do you get off thinking you…?'

'Let's cut to the chase; you can reach for the outrage later in your own time. For now, I'll present the advantages. You will accept my proposal to become Mrs Cayetano Figueroa with all the advantages that involves. In return, we will marry in two weeks.'

CHAPTER THREE

BENEATH THE CHANDELIER lights of his dining room, Cayetano watched the parade of emotions race across his PA's face, with emotion that should've been a lot more detached than it was. As for the anticipatory breath currently locked in his solar plexus...

That, he told himself, was merely the urgency to lock down at least one thing—one important thing. Without it, everything he'd worked for, since he'd been old enough to assume even the most menial responsibility within the company his grandfather had built from nothing, would be worthless.

It didn't escape him that it was the old man who'd put him in this position in the first place. After an exhaustive twelve months without finding a loophole, Cayetano had begrudgingly accepted that this was his only path. So, yes, he was interested in her every reaction to his proposal.

What he hadn't expected was what it turned out to be: bafflement; disbelief; panicked amusement; cynicism. Then...*outrage*?

That, he accepted with a punch of surprise, was unexpected. He could claim without an ounce of conceit that no woman had ever expressed outrage at anything he'd demanded, through word or deed. The unprecedented reaction held his tongue hostage as she sucked in a sharp breath.

'Mr Figueroa—'

'If we're going to be man and wife, you need to adjust yourself to calling me Cayetano. Or Caye if it pleases you,' he tacked on after a moment's thought. Why, exactly, he wasn't entirely sure. Very few people addressed him that informally, and most of those were blood relatives.

'Mr Figueroa,' she insisted, her hazel eyes now sparking with irritation, while still reflecting several layers of shock. 'If this is some sort of practical joke, then okay, you got me. Ha-ha!'

'It is not. I can guarantee that.'

Why was it that he didn't mind that flash of fire at his interruption? *Dios mio*, didn't he have enough on his plate? Hadn't he, just ten short minutes ago, divested himself of another spirited candidate? And one he hadn't had the insane inclination to touch or kiss or *savour* the way he did this one.

Hell, the faintest twinge of regret about getting rid of Octavia as his fiancée had already vanished. Despite her melodramatic and demanding tendencies, she was a hell of a PA, her ability to navigate the sometimes delicate avenues of the corporate world when his patience was frayed quite exemplary—not to mention her very useful pedigree.

But...

'Then I'm afraid I'll have to decline this...interesting offer.'

Insane—she meant insane. The word had all but screamed from her quivering voice when she'd uttered the word 'interesting'. And, from the bewildered look in her eyes as she examined him, she thought he'd taken leave of his senses.

Perhaps he had.

But she hadn't taken the exquisite diamond ring off her finger…yet. Nor had she stopped tracing the edges with her thumb every few seconds.

Did she even know she was doing that? Did she know she wore her every emotion on her face? That, when she'd announced she wasn't his type, the pulse had been leaping at her throat and her alluring eyes had all but *devoured* his mouth?

With every fibre of his being, he yearned to demonstrate to her how utterly useless her protests were. But he'd *never* taken what wasn't freely given. Until she gave him the answer he sought, he had to maintain strict professional barriers. Hell, even then, whatever interactions came after would be strictly for appearances' sake.

The reminder that this was far from an emotional match, the kind he had no intention of indulging in any time soon—perhaps ever—cauterised his wandering thoughts. She'd said no…while she caressed his ring. Perhaps he could incentivise her.

Money and wealth were powerful influencers. As the controller of his parents' purse strings, he knew that bitter truth all too well. He could catalogue on the fingers of one hand the times either of his parents had contacted him *without* financial scrounging having motivated them.

'If it sways you, you can keep that ring. You seemed very enamoured of it earlier this evening, if I recall.'

Cayetano watched her dazed glance drop to the ring, then back again, anger morphing into awe. 'What? Did you just say…?'

'*Si*, you heard right.'

'But…it's priceless.'

His lips twisted. 'Hardly. It's unique and quite magnificent—you should commend yourself for choosing it—but it's far from priceless. I'm yet to receive the exact figure but I believe, since Miss Smythe's pieces start from a million at least, the ring on your finger is worth at least three million.'

Her gasp was sweet and sultry, sexy but strangely innocent in a way that made Caye yearn to hear it again. *And again.* Hell, if it wasn't as contrived as he suspected, she would be eaten alive in the shark-infested, corporate waters of Buenos Aires.

Tightening his gut against the resurgence of the libidinous heat he'd experienced at Smythe's, he watched her alarmed gaze dart back to the ring.

'No way!'

'Oh, yes.'

'And she just let you walk out with a ring worth that much?'

'Perhaps because she knew I value integrity more than most characteristics and won't attempt anything underhanded. Which is why you should reconsider my proposal, Miss Dixon.'

As much as the circumstances infuriated him, it was the time for the 'honey not vinegar' approach. Although, that sage internal counselling fractured when she shook her head again.

'Even if I wanted to consider this…this *proposal*…' She spat the word as if it was offensive, and Cayetano made a mental note to pay her back for that at some point in the future. 'I feel like you've skipped several vital steps.'

Her hands waved expressively as she spoke—another first he noted. Seriously, at this point he was wondering if he was dealing with a split personality—the spirited siren versus the level-headed PA. And, *Dios*, his body knew which it preferred.

But her observation sobered him. Glancing at the table, he saw her half-finished meal.

'Sit down, Mareka.'

Her blatant suspicion ratcheted up his irritation.

'You claim you haven't eaten since breakfast. I interrupted your meal and I want you clear-headed for this next bit.'

Her lips pursed, instantly drawing his attention to their plump curves. To his eternal relief, she took the seat but, though she reached for her cutlery, she didn't eat, instead sending him furtive glances from beneath her lush eyelashes. Glances that held flashes of innocence he wanted to explore far more than was wise. He suppressed the absurd need and served himself a cut of the prime Argentinian steak that usually improved his mood.

He took a bite and chewed, although the satisfaction in this instance was marginal. Cayetano suspected nothing would elevate his mood short of a stone-carved assurance that his birthright was intact. 'To summarise—I have to marry before my thirty-fifth birthday to secure the company I've spent almost twenty years devoting myself to.'

'You mean Figueroa Industries?'

'Si,' he responded, the very act of confirming this ridiculous situation threatening to blacken his mood once more.

'Why? You're already the CEO.'

The meat congealed in his mouth, the very idea of having to say this out loud sticking in his craw. 'My grandfather created a stipulation in his will that demanded that every CEO, male or female, needed to be married by their thirty-fifth birthday to keep the position. It's a clause that has withstood vigorous opposition—including mine.'

While he'd loved his grandfather, he'd contested the constraining clause on principle. That it was one of the very few battles Cayetano had lost was a failure that wasn't easy to swallow.

'Why would he do that?'

Cayetano resisted the urge to grind his teeth. It would earn him a trip to the dentist and not much else. 'Because my grandfather believed that a married CEO would make a better leader than a single one,' he supplied with a bite of bitterness he couldn't avoid.

Wide hazel eyes regarded him with practised aloofness. 'You don't share that view, obviously.'

There was no point denying it. 'No, I do not.' The words were cold, detached—exactly how he felt about tying himself to another person in the name of some lofty emotion that rarely lasted a week, never mind a lifetime.

His grandparents might have beaten the odds to sustain a union that had lasted decades, but Cayetano suspected it hadn't been without its challenges, no matter how the old man had loved to boast. That he'd passed within a month of Cayetano's grandmother's death, supposedly from a broken heart, was a mournful but wistful tale some family members liked to regale to suit their own blinkered outlook.

He knew better... Hell, he'd *lived* the truth. He'd seen his parents drop even the pretence of a united front and collapse into all-out war long before he'd shed his baby teeth. And still his grandfather had insisted on some farcical 'one true love' myth. So Cayetano had been practical and put it to the test. To say he'd come up shockingly short was the understatement of the century.

What he'd discovered instead—through a series of relationships in his twenties his grandfather had laughingly dismissed as him sowing his wild oats—were the many tools available to dismantle even the staunchest of unions: infidelity; apathy; cruelty; mistrust.

And the recurring theme of good, old-fashioned greed. He'd been scrupulous about laying all his cards on the table since then. No woman who'd graced his arm or his bed since he'd hit the milestone age of thirty could have accused him of misleading them or misrepresenting his intentions.

And he intended to deal with his PA in the same vein. He refocused on her, to glimpse something shadowed and surprisingly bleak pass through her eyes.

'With respect to everything you've said, and appreciating the dilemma you're in…' she paused, swiped her tongue over her lower lip before continuing '…what makes you think I'll accept a ring you chose for another woman?'

And there it was—one of those obstacles created by unnecessary emotional attachment. He suppressed a sigh. 'But I didn't choose it, did I, Mareka?'

The noise she made when he uttered her name sent another lance of heat straight to his groin. *Maldita sea!* He really needed to find time to blow off steam if simple things like his hitherto unflappable PA's reaction to his uttering her name made him think of sweaty sheets and the sublime sensation of a woman's nails scoring down his back.

He needed a few rounds in the boxing ring with his personal trainer. Maybe a skydiving trip in his beloved Andes. Or even a good old-fashioned sex marathon with a woman who knew and accepted the 'sex only' score.

After he'd done away with this rose-coloured glasses nonsense and secured Mareka's agreement to his proposal.

'*You* chose it. Out of the selection you created for me, this was the one you favoured above all else. True or false?'

She wanted to protest, but she knew he spoke the truth. Her lips firmed and she remained silent. He pressed on, wanting this over as quickly as possible.

'I watched you at Smythe's for a few minutes before you noticed me.'

And he'd learned a few surprising things about the PA whose efficiency impressed him but whose unobtrusive presence had made her almost forgettable.

Until that night in Italy…and tonight.

'You're a hopeless romantic,' he declared without inflexion or judgement. He didn't care either way. All he cared about was her cooperation with his plans.

Heat and outrage surged into her face. 'I…' She paused, then her chin lifted. 'So what if I am? The way I feel about…certain things…hasn't affected my job, so I'm not even sure why you're bringing it up.'

'I'm bringing it up because it will expedite you accepting that ring you're reluctant to take off your finger. So can we cut through the bull and get on with it?'

'Why are we still even discussing this when I've already given my answer?'

He allowed himself a smug but resigned little smile and pulled out the big guns. 'Did I mention the one million pounds that will be deposited in your bank account if you accept my proposal?' he slid in smoothly.

And watched her eyes turn into wide saucers.

She'd misheard him. 'I… What?'

'Marry me and, on our wedding day, you'll receive

one million pounds free and clear,' he enunciated slowly, clearly, as if he doubted her hearing.

Mareka glanced around the room, wondering if she'd slid down some rabbit hole without realising it. Nope, she was still in his penthouse. The view in the distance still showed the glittering lights of London. 'I heard you the first time, Mr Figueroa. What I meant was...'

She snatched in a breath, much like she'd been doing ever since he'd walked into the room and announced his absurd proposal. When she couldn't quite catch her breath, she shook her head. 'It doesn't even matter *why*. I don't want or need your money.'

Not entirely true. Think of how that could accelerate your goals.

One eyebrow arched; dear God, why did every motion make him even more breath-taking? 'Nonsense. Everyone wants money,' he delivered with bone-dry cynicism. 'On very rare occasions, not for themselves, but for someone else they care about. Not even saints turn down money.'

'And you're familiar with saints, are you?' she snapped before she could stop herself, then lowered her gaze as his glinted with the beginning of a blaze she was a little terrified to watch directly.

'Not from personal experience, but I'm sure there are reams written about them seeking patrons for practical causes on behalf of lost souls. And guess who made that happen?'

Her gaze flicked up and was immediately captured by his. 'Men like you?'

'Indeed. So, you see, even saints need men like me.' His gaze left hers and conducted a lazy survey of her body while his luscious mouth twisted. 'And you'll have a hell of a time convincing me you're a saint,' he murmured, his sexy drawl making her belly clench and heat pool in between her legs.

This shouldn't be happening. Not when she'd so efficiently talked herself out of her foolish crush on her boss. Not when she'd vowed to maintain the utmost professionalism the next time Cayetano Figueroa graced his London headquarters with his presence. 'I can't. I work for you. This is—'

'Another role that will earn you a salary.' His gaze dropped to the ring. 'And benefits you'd probably never see in this lifetime.'

'I'm sure you think your offer should impress me, but don't you think you're being presumptuous by assuming I won't earn that kind of money on my own *in this lifetime*?'

A hard smile played at his lips. Then he strolled towards her. 'I started working in my grandfather's company as an errand boy in the staff kitchen. He refused to allow me to use my real name because he didn't want me getting preferential treatment. Do you know what that taught me, Mareka?'

'That, regardless of whatever lesson he taught you, you would still inherit the throne one day?'

His face hardened. 'No. It taught me not to be too proud to accept opportunities when they came my way. In whatever form they arrived in.' He leaned in closer, looking her in the eye. 'Are you really going to walk away from potential millions?' he taunted with a near-whisper.

A near-whisper that screamed in her head in the silence that ensued. Because, now she'd heard the offer for the third…or was it the fourth?…time, the shock was clearing and paving way for the dream she'd yearned for and dismissed as impossible. A dream that would require a miracle to turn into reality.

He's offering that miracle.

But at what cost? Not to mention…what would her parents think?

Mareka shied away from that thought for the simple fact that it didn't bear thinking about. They would condemn her whatever decision she made. Not that she was considering it…was she?

She shook her head, desperate for a clear path through her rumbled thoughts. 'I should go.'

Cayetano's eyes narrowed. 'Go where, exactly?'

'Home. Where else?'

'Do you think that's wise?' he enquired.

She frowned. 'Why wouldn't it be?'

Moss-green eyes regarded her steadily. 'You've been photographed in my arms, wearing my ring. Do you really think the luxury of privacy is still yours?'

'They don't know where I live,' she protested, alarm leeching through her voice.

That eyebrow arched again. 'You want to bet?'

The silky question made panic surge through her. Glancing round, Mareka dashed across the room to where she'd left her handbag. Grabbing her phone, she activated her video doorbell, eager to prove to him that she'd been a nobody this morning, and she still was.

A gasp leapt free of her throat when she saw the live feed of her front door. A dozen strangers—at least— wielding cameras prowled just beyond the small patch of lawn that fronted her ground-floor flat. As she watched, one bolshie character pranced down the stone path and leaned on the bell. The jangle echoed through her phone, making her jump.

'I suggest you turn that off and leave it off for the time being.' Cayetano's breath rushing over her earlobe caused shivers all over again. 'And that's an order from your boss. Because, in case you've forgotten, you were supposed to make yourself available to me this evening anyway, were you not?'

'To assist you with Figueroa Industries matters, not...'

'Being presented with an opportunity you're still too prideful to grasp? And, before you spew further inane protests, look me in the eye and tell me you have no use for what I'm offering.'

She...couldn't. Now the seed had taken root, she couldn't shake it. She knew deep in her soul that rejecting it out of hand without further thought would haunt her for ever. She could help *so many people* with that money.

But at what cost?

The question returned, stronger.

'I need to think about—'

'No. I don't have time to waste. My New York lawyers are on standby. If your name isn't going on the contract, I'd like to know tonight.'

'You already have a contract drawn up?' She frowned, then answered her own question. 'Of course you do. Could this be more clinical if you tried?'

'You disadvantage yourself and me by believing this is anything but a business transaction. I'm purchasing your services for a finite amount of time, Mareka. Imagining anything else is ill-advised.'

Something hard and rough twisted in her chest. She pushed it away, just as she'd pushed away every impossible thought surrounding Cayetano Figueroa. As much as it burned to hear it, he was right. Hadn't she admonished herself for that very same notion minutes ago?

A business transaction. That was all this was. All it could ever be. And, when it was done, when she'd fulfilled her end of the bargain, she could fulfil her lifelong dream. Prove to her parents that she wasn't a hopeless cause after all. And if they continued to believe that...

She shrugged. She would live her life for herself. She would hold her head high and revel in her achievements.

'You should know by now that I'm not a man who likes to be kept waiting,' Cayetano bit out.

She focused on him—on this man who intended to pluck her off his corporate shelf and put a ring on her finger. This man who'd looked at her and seen her as nothing but a replacement for another woman.

She would do well to take a leaf out of his book. Be cold and detached and seize an opportunity for the sake of every young person who needed a helping hand, be it financial or psychological.

Wasn't it ironic that, despite his warning to keep emotion out of this, that was what would grant her emotional satisfaction somewhere in her near future?

Yes. It was.

Welcoming the layer of balm that thought provided, she raised her head and looked him in the eye. And, despite the wild drumming of her heart and churning in the region of her heart, she shrugged and said, 'Congratulations, Mr Figueroa. You've just earned yourself a business partner.'

CHAPTER FOUR

YOU'VE JUST EARNED yourself a business partner.

Her words didn't sit well with him—not when she uttered them, or in the hours that followed. Her mercurial transformation from shock, being almost nonplussed and showing outright rejection to cool, professional acquiescence rubbed something raw and uncomfortable inside him. Something that would be diffused with sleep, he concluded at two a.m., when a ping on his phone signalled yet another helpful 'suggestion' from his lawyer on how best to further constrain the woefully scant demands of his PA.

He passed a hand over his gritty eyes and frowned.

Cayetano hadn't expected her to drive negotiations as hard as Octavia had, but neither had he expected her to have so few demands, especially considering the matter-of-fact way she'd accepted his proposal. Her main stipulation had been to reduce the length of their convenience marriage from four years to three. Which should have suited him just fine.

Except… He rubbed his chest, the chafing digging in deeper, eluding his attempts to eradicate it.

'Are we done?'

His gaze snapped up from where her feet rested on the sofa.

At some point she'd taken off her shoes and got more comfortable as she read the contract. Cayetano hadn't drawn her attention to it. He had been far too captivated by her smoothly arched feet and her slim, delicate, perfectly grabbable ankles. It wasn't a stretch at all to imagine himself between them, gripping tight as he thrust hard and…

'Mr… Cayetano? What are you doing?'

He jerked, looked down and realised his finger was stroking the arch of her foot. *Dios*. Had he lost every crumb of sanity?

He clenched his traitorous hand into a fist and started to withdraw. But then the sometimes-innocent, sometimes-siren who'd confounded him since he'd walked into the secret diamond boutique in Knightsbridge floored him. She moved her foot *into* his hold, a soft moan escaping her plump lips as their skin brushed.

His snatched-in breath stalled in his lung as he watched the pen tumble from her fingers to the floor, their marriage contract slithering after it. He watched her chest rise and fall in seductive, arousing agitation. His fingers unfurled. He gripped the enticing ankle and tugged it until her legs parted. Until that maddening little pencil skirt inched up her smooth thighs.

He stopped then, trying to regain some semblance of control. But she moved again. *Moaned* again. A pulse fluttered at her throat.

And Cayetano… Dear God, he was *enthralled*.

He parted her legs, made space for himself and, as her alluring eyes locked on his, he pressed her back against the sofa, his lower body fusing with hers as he gave into the craving and tasted that maddening pulse at her neck.

Santo cielo! Her skin tasted like sin and heaven. He wanted to gorge on both! He found her perfect breasts and toyed with her nipple until her back arched. Then he moved lower, the centre of her a siren's call he was too weak to refuse. A hoarse groan tore from him as he yanked up her skirt, his fingers delving beneath her panties to discover...

'*Dios mio*...how wet you are for me.' He grunted against her lips, drawing back to watch her as he caressed the heart of her.

A deep flush suffused her cheeks, a soft mewl falling from her as he plunged one finger inside her.

'Oh, God, please. I'm... I'm...'

He surged forward, still high on madness, ready to give them both what they craved.

Another ping sounded from his phone. Mareka's fingers froze on his shoulders, her eyes widening in alarm. Then she shoved at his shoulders.

Cayetano jerked backwards, shock duelling with thwarted need as he stared down at her. Sweet heaven, what had he done?

He had truly lost his mind.

Even accepting that, he couldn't stop looking at her. Couldn't stop his gaze from dropping to the heart of her—the *damp* heart of her.

He surged and whirled away from pure temptation, his erection straining painfully. Dragging his fingers through his hair, he placed vital distance between them and cleared his throat.

'That was—'

'Something I want to forget ever happened,' she whispered, her voice husky and shaky, affronted.

His jaw tightened. He wanted to tell her he wouldn't forget it any time soon. That even now he could barely restrain himself from finishing what he...*they*...had started.

But Cayetano knew when retreat was better in battle. So he wrested back his control and nodded briskly. 'Agreed.'

He turned round just as she wrestled her own bewilderment, her eyes sweeping away from his as she scooped up the document and pen.

'You have a list of our UK legal counsel, I'm sure. Arrange for one of them to come here first thing in the morning to witness the signing.'

She nodded and Caye just about managed to keep his gaze from shifting to the rich, dark-gold curls bouncing over her shoulders. To the gap in her shirt granting him a tantalising view of her breasts.

He most definitely wasn't going to think about how it would feel to shove his fingers into that glorious mass, feel its silky weight on his skin and grip it tightly to tilt her head so he could read her every expression. So they could both savour what came next.

'Okay.' She sucked her lips between her teeth for a fraction of a second, during which heat flashed through his groin. 'What happens after that?'

His disgruntlement at his body's relentless reaction to her bled through his brusque reply. 'Then you get to sit back and reap the rewards of your bargain. Who knows? You might even thank me for the honour of becoming Mrs Cayetano Figueroa.'

He strode away, ignoring the flash of hurt on her face and the stinging sensation that all of this was getting to him far too much. That he would love nothing better than to wipe the last twenty-four hours out of existence.

In his bedroom, he stopped in the middle of the room, teeth gritted. It was a waste of energy to curse his dead grandfather or to feel guilty that, had the old man been alive, he would've been disappointed by Cayetano's vigorous opposition of his demand.

But how could he not have done so when he'd lived with the very brazen evidence of marriage failure in his childhood? When even now he witnessed his mother's bitterness far too frequently, expressed in acerbic outbursts every time they were within speaking distance?

Basta. Enough.

He'd found himself a convenient wife to secure his birthright. So what if he couldn't shake the notion that this decision would trigger challenges down the line? That what seemed like an easier outcome than he'd anticipated might turn out too good to be true?

Whatever. He wouldn't be where he was today if he shied away in the face of challenges, big and small. Whatever came next, he would deal with it, just like he'd dealt with everything in his life—with cold, strategic, emotionless thinking that ultimately got him what he wanted.

Mareka held her phone to her ear, listening to the ring with growing dread. She'd stumbled into bed after that incident on the sofa, her needy body raging war with her stunned mind, despair nipping hard at her heels.

She couldn't believe what she'd allowed to happen, and how easily she'd fallen into temptation the second Cayetano had touched her. Maybe she was as rudderless as her parents accused her of.

No. She killed the thought, but her stomach continued to churn.

They'd stopped before they crossed a line.

Even though he had his fingers inside you?

Heat storming her body, threatening to rile up that need once more, she willed the phone to be answered. She'd risen bleary-eyed after a restless night, to the alarmed horror that she'd forgotten one vital thing—informing her parents of the decision she'd made last night.

Her father had his one and only cup of coffee while catching up on current affairs at six a.m. so he could discourse with her mother when she woke at seven. It was now six-fifteen. And her parents weren't answering her call.

Dread charted a slow, taunting trajectory through her chest. It was foolish to hope her parents hadn't seen the picture from yesterday. They were far too regimented to deviate from their morning routine without just cause, and this morning Mareka suspected that cause was her. Even across the miles, their disappointment weighed heavily.

'Yes?'

She jack-knifed in bed at her father's crisp greeting. 'Hi, Dad, it's me.'

'Yes, I'm aware,' he said. The extra-chilled tone confirmed her worst fears.

'I… I have some news. Is Mum around?' She'd rather get this over with in one go.

'She's here. You're on speaker.'

Mareka opened her mouth, but every word that formed in her brain seemed nonsensical, trite. It was a rash middle-of-the-night decision made entirely from believing she could go toe-to-toe with an enigmatic billionaire whose charisma and intelligence often left her slack-jawed.

Concentrate on the end goal—how much you'll be helping those who need it most.

'I'm…getting married. To the man I work… To my boss, Cayetano Figueroa,' she eventually blurted, sticking to the bare facts. They appreciated that more often than not.

Except the arctic silence that ensued made her wonder if she should've tried for a little embellishment. Such as, she'd once had a secret crush on the same boss she'd agreed to marry so he could secure his company? Or that her first emotion when he'd proposed had been a nanosecond of unadulterated joy before reality had killed it dead?

She could say none of that, of course. For starters, she'd agreed to keep every aspect bar the news that they were marrying strictly confidential. Plus, she wasn't about to hand her parents another reason to label her a disappointment.

The silence stretched, as did Mareka's nerves. 'I know it seems rash and rushed...' She trailed off, cringing at handing them the perfect rod with which to whip her. Her father's response didn't disappoint.

'What else is new?' Lately, they didn't even bother to curtail their disdain.

'Have you got yourself pregnant?' That bald, coldly snapped question came from her mother, disappointment already staining her voice.

'What? Of course not!' But, despite her protest, she was stingingly reminded of why her mother would reach for that supposition. After all, it had been a similar *unplanned* dilemma that had produced Mareka.

An impatient huff burst from the phone. 'Your outrage is misplaced, young lady, considering you've been photographed with him in a compromised position and are calling the next morning with this...highly questionable news.'

She fought off a cringe that her parents had already seen the pictures.

Brush off the hurt. Don't take the bait. Don't take the...

'Why is it questionable? Because you think a girl like

me can't land a man like Cayetano Figueroa?' Even as the words left her mouth, Mareka regretted them.

Sure enough, another canyon of silence stretched between them, one her parents didn't hurry to break.

'I'm sorry,' Mareka offered, even as bitterness filled the stretch. She'd been apologising for one thing or another for as long as she could remember. When would she learn that engaging only led to hurt?

Because they're my parents. It's not normal to be made to feel like this.

Futile tears building at the back of her throat—because, no matter how hard she tried, the hurt never went away—she cleared it quickly.

'It's early days, so no firm plans have been made,' she said, swiftly straightening the fingers beginning to cross on the silky duvet. 'I'll let you know when that changes, if you want?' She hated herself for the hope that tinged her voice.

One beat passed, then two.

'That would be welcome. We wouldn't want to be any more embarrassed if we're found not to know the details of our own daughter's nuptials, would we?' her father enquired coolly. 'Now, we must get on with our day before our schedule is further disrupted. Goodbye, Mareka.'

Her murmured response bounced off the dead line. Dejection attempted to creep into her chest. Tossing the phone away, she forcefully ejected herself from bed, as if doing so would disperse the fog shrouding ever closer.

Brisk strides took her to the spotless, luxurious bathroom. She wrenched the shower tap with more vigour than was necessary. But stepping beneath the hot spray and angling her face up to the wet needles didn't dispel the fact that tears were spilling. That, once again, the parents who should love her, or at the very least *care* for her, had made her feel inconsequential and hopeless. An inconvenience they couldn't wait to be rid of.

Her parents had been careless with birth control and had regretfully reaped the consequences on their honeymoon—a caustic fact meticulously recorded by her mother in her diary and discovered by Mareka when she'd been the tender age of nine.

Robert and I agree that nothing will change. This is simply another task to be managed.

Her mother's words were seared on Mareka's psyche for ever. Did she wish she'd never given in to curiosity and peeked in the diary her mother wrote in every night before dinner? *Yes.* But at least she'd finally understood why her parents were so cold and indifferent towards her.

Mareka scrubbed at her eyes, impatient with herself for picking at old wounds. She'd done her duty and told them, just as she would do her duty and honour the agreement with Cayetano. All she needed to do was remind herself of the rewards she would be reaping.

In a matter of weeks, she could be on her way to setting up her charity, helping displaced young people find their place in the world. For now, though, she needed to face Cayetano, the man who'd reawakened so many forbidden cravings in her last night.

Mareka wrenched the tap to cold when her body started to heat up once more. Ten minutes later, confident she was once more under control, she grimaced at the thought of wearing yesterday's clothes, then got on with it.

She entered the living room at the stroke of seven. Only to stop short at the sight of Cayetano sitting at the dining table, fully dressed, a tablet at his elbow as he enjoyed a poached egg and the specially cured Argentinian ham she took pains to ensure was on hand whenever he visited England.

His gaze flicked up in a searing once-over before returning to the screen. *'Buenos días.'*

'Good morning,' she murmured, a little thrown that he was addressing her in his mother tongue when he never had before.

'You should learn rudimentary Spanish if we're to go ahead with this.'

Something snagged in her midriff, then triggered a dreadful little tremor through her frame. 'If?' The question emerged tight and hoarse, not at all showing the composure she desperately sought. She took a breath, then blurted entirely against her will, 'Are you having second thoughts?'

His eyebrows rose, as if she'd surprised him. A second later, he set down his fork and sat back. 'On the contrary, that *if* was directed at you. I've been reminded very recently that women are prone to changing their minds faster than a speeding bullet,' he stated drily, with the edge that seemed never far away.

Hard on the heels of having her parents call her character into question, Cayetano's veiled vilification landed like a slap. Her fists bunched at her sides before she could will them not to. Another step closer to the table, and she was near enough to smell his aftershave, close enough to see the tiny flecks in his eyes. She hated herself for noticing these things about him, just as she hated herself for the emotions she couldn't keep bottled down.

'I'd thank you not to tar me with the same brush as your other women. Surely you're experienced enough to know no woman likes to be compared to another, especially one her future husband had a connection with? How would you react if I compared you to a boyfriend?'

His eyes flared, then his face tightened. 'Not favourably. And most definitely if it was a present one.'

She heard the clear question in his response but refused to give him the satisfaction of an answer. Instead, she arched her brows, her fists remaining tight despite the composure she willed into her being.

For an age, they stared each other down, then his gaze travelled down to her clenched fists, the tiniest twitch lifting the corners of his mouth. 'I don't recall you displaying such fierceness before,' he mused. 'But you have my apologies for causing offence.'

A little mollified, Mareka breathed out, ignoring the tiny voice wondering if she'd overreacted a touch. 'Apology accepted,' she muttered.

His gaze remained on her for another stretch, then he rose fluidly to his feet. Her breath caught in her throat as he took a single step towards her, swallowing the gap between then. Feeling her pulse skitter wildly, Mareka was about to ask what he was doing when he reached around and pulled out her chair.

'Oh, I...thanks,' she said, further cringing at how he so casily left her tongue tied. How, for a moment, she'd thought there was to be a version of last night played out.

'De nada,' he said, his voice low, deep and sending shivers down her spine.

She was lamenting just how dismayingly clichéd it was for her to find his Argentinian accent so sexy when a butler glided in, thankfully saving her from doing something stupid.

Mareka grabbed the chance to clear her mind of everything that had happened in the last few minutes and to distance herself from the searing jealousy she'd experienced when Cayetano had compared her to the woman he'd intended to marry only a few short hours ago.

It was merely an aberration, a remnant of emotions she'd had no business feeling in the first place. But a few sips of coffee and a couple of mouthfuls of delicious muesli and she was once again hot and bothered, Cayetano's gaze having returned to examine her.

'W-what?' she stuttered.

'You're yet to answer me.'

She flailed around for several seconds before she remembered. 'Oh. Well, I haven't changed my mind. I tend to keep my promises.' Such as the one she'd made to herself a handful of years after reading that diary entry— that she wouldn't spend her life feeling like a spare part. More importantly, she'd ensure she helped other women feel the same as she wanted to.

Last night, despite his left-field proposal, Cayetano Figueroa had propelled her towards keeping that promise.

'Is that so?' came the silky reply.

'I haven't let you down so far, have I?'

He shrugged. 'Professionally, no. Your work is exemplary. But this assignment requires exceptional attention to detail.'

'Such as?'

'Such as knowing each other to a level that will ensure we pass muster where it matters.'

She stiffened. Was that what the sofa incident last night had been about—a test of her mettle? 'What does that mean, exactly? Who do we have to prove our relationship to—the papers?'

'What the tabloids report of me is of very little relevance,' he answered in a clipped tone. Before she could remind him that it had seemed quite the opposite last night, he continued. 'My inner circle back in Argentina and several key people need to believe that our marriage is real, not a paper-only contract.'

She frowned, a part of her feeling that tremor again. 'You didn't say any of this last night.'

He gave another shrug. 'I didn't see the point in overwhelming you with too much detail.'

Pique ruffled her nape. 'I'm not a hothouse flower you need to coddle, you know?'

'Good, then you won't clutch your pearls or protest when I touch you or kiss you in public.'

Her next swallow of coffee went down the wrong way, triggering a fit of coughing. 'Did you wait until after I agreed to marry you to spell out those...*addendums*?' she demanded when she'd caught her breath.

'Does it matter?'

'Of course it matters! We'll be... You're asking me for...intimacy. Was last night...?'

'Last night was, as we both agreed, a late-night aberration.' Something dark and secret passed through his eyes, gone before she could plant an accurate label on it. Still, she grew hotter when his gaze dropped to linger on her mouth. 'Considering how much I'm paying you, a small show for appearances isn't much to ask.'

A small show that would involve them touching. That risked her betraying her indecent craving. 'To you, maybe. Not to me. You're paying me to act as your wife. You're not buying my body or my...my...' She floundered, the reminder of his hands on her, *inside her*, stirring her temperature, all while he sat in his chair, the picture of composure. 'You should have told me this last night.'

'Hmm. It seems we're either at an impasse or this is a deal-breaker for you. Which is it, Mareka?'

The way he said her name, with an emphasis on the 'r', sent another wavelet of heat through her belly. She suppressed the sensation while struggling to look away from the lips that uttered it, the sensual curve of it, the way it was now slightly pursed as he watched her with narrow-eyed intent. The thought of kissing those lips in public, even for the benefit of their ruse, made her heart hammer and her pulse spike even harder.

That was out of the question, of course. But…maybe it didn't have to be his way or the highway. 'I propose a compromise.'

'*Si?*'

God, she really needed to get over this belly-flip every time he spoke Spanish. 'I agree to…um…a small degree of touching, but no kissing…on the lips. That's my final word on it.' Considering what they'd done last night, it was probably a ridiculous request to him; but she'd fantasised about kissing this man for so long, she knew deep in her bones she would be lost if that became a reality. Especially a reality that was only a means to an end for him.

His eyes glinted, wicked, earthy and, oh, so cynical. His fingers reached out, plucked his coffee cup from its saucer and downed the remaining contents. He set it back down, all without taking his eyes off her. She was fighting the urge to squirm beneath that raw gaze when he said, 'I'm beginning to wonder at your level of experience, Mareka.'

'What do you mean?'

His amusement intensified, sardonic humour lighting his eyes. 'I mean, I wonder if you've known the true touch of a man if you think kissing on the lips is the height of intimacy you can achieve with your clothes on.'

Heat surged up her face so fiercely, her skin tingled with the force of it. 'I don't—'

'It's okay, you don't need to defend your stance. I accept your offer.'

He held out his hand to her.

And in that moment, torn between taking back words she suspected had just landed her into an unforeseen quagmire and congratulating herself for not blowing her chance, she felt the earth shake and tilt beneath her feet.

But…what was the worst that could happen?

She got her first taster when she sucked in a breath, placed her hand in his and watched him tug it firmly but gently towards him before brushing those lips over it, lips she'd daydreamed about only a minute ago. Panic made her stomach dip, roll and drop like a rollercoaster before surging back up to drive the breath out of her lungs.

Cayetano released her almost immediately.

But the impression he'd left—that he could set her body alight with just a simple touch—lingered long after the lawyers arrived and she signed the documents committing her to three years as Mrs Cayetano Figueroa.

Some time later, he officially slipped the engagement ring onto her finger and had a car drive her home to pack her bags so they could leave for Buenos Aires early that evening.

CHAPTER FIVE

THE WEDDING TOOK place two weeks and one day later at Cayetano's private estate just outside Buenos Aires. Mareka barely caught her breath in all that time. Every time she'd thought she had five minutes to herself, some sleekly dressed assistant, event co-ordinator or haute couture designer *simply had to have* her input on one thing or another.

She'd accepted a mere three days after their whirlwind arrival that perhaps she would've been better off not trying to compete with the other staggering parts of Caye's empire—especially the Argentinians.

The London and European offices easily employed a thousand people. While she'd known Argentina was where Figueroa Industries had been started by Caye's grandfather, Mareka hadn't quite grasped that Figueroa Industries employed close to twenty-five thousand in South America alone, with only a fraction less in the States. And that the inner circle and key people Cayetano had spoken of numbered several dozen, all clamouring to meet their CEO's new wife.

She'd attended more dinners, garden and cocktail parties and galas in the last two weeks than in her entire life so far.

Which brought her to why her heart continued to twist even now, the night before her wedding, when she'd finally been left alone by the co-ordinator. The older woman had stated plainly that she didn't want a tired bride ruining the wedding photos and risking the spotlight being taken off the wedding dress. Mareka had been too shocked by the blunt statement to do more than smile and escape to her private suite.

But, while she could console herself with knowing she wouldn't have to see a large proportion of the organisers after tomorrow, the people she would have to see again were her parents.

Mareka had thought of their arrival two nights ago, and the quietly icy disapproval they'd displayed all through the private pre-dinner drinks she'd hosted with Cayetano in his Buenos Aires penthouse, would be the height of her anxiety.

She'd been wrong.

Somehow, Cayetano had withstood her parents' near-monosyllabic non-engagement for all of ten minutes before he'd launched into a charm offensive, systematically dismantling their icy demeanours with a focus that had been disarming and spellbinding to watch.

Her jaw had almost dropped when she'd discovered Caye knew the ins and outs of her parents' careers, engaging them and drawing them out with astute and challenging conversation they'd latched onto, easily extending the two hours she'd intended for the ordeal into three and a half.

Watching her parents fall under her future husband's spell had filled her with a feeling she couldn't quite describe—something like pride, but not quite, since that would be misplaced; Cayetano Figueroa wasn't *hers* to be proud of. The darts of jealousy seemed petty, considering Caye had singlehandedly turned a much-dreaded ordeal into a passably pleasant evening. She'd settled on gratitude as her parents had bid them goodnight. Her mother's gaze had lingered on Mareka with a look that had skated the very outer rim of approval before the cold indifference had slotted back into place.

Fortunately, or unfortunately, that sliver of approval had lowered her guard, enough that she'd been disarmed and dismayed when her mother's text had arrived just before she'd gone to bed last night.

I require five minutes of your time before the wedding. Mother.

No matter how many times she told herself her parents would be gone this time tomorrow, she couldn't shake the renewed anxiety swirling through her.

Or the fact that it had only exacerbated the dismay at the new facet of Cayetano's treatment. Since their arrival, he'd stuck to their strict agreement that any physical contact between them be minimal. While Mareka was glad of it—*she needed to be*—the last thing she'd expected was the coldly neutral dismissal that came with it.

At first, she'd been sure it was her imagination, that her hang-ups from her parents were spilling over into her thoughts about Cayetano's interaction with her. But two weeks of standing next to him and smiling for the cameras, after which he'd treated her with stiff formality bordering on apathy, had opened a vein of despair she couldn't seem to suppress.

On top of that was Mareka's other problem. The insanely breathtaking PA and *almost* fiancée whose place

Mareka had taken. She had assumed—wrongly, it turned out—that Caye's Argentinian PA would interact with her boss only during business hours, perhaps even choosing to stay out of sight altogether. But the statuesque beauty had made an appearance at every notable occasion so far.

Rational deduction suggested it was to have been expected, since a quick Internet search had revealed that Octavia Morena and her family were powerful and influential, highly regarded in Buenos Aires. That, even before she'd taken the role as Caye's assistant, she'd been part of his inner circle, their association going back to adolescence.

If Mareka had expected the other woman to be upset about ending her agreement to marry her boss, she'd been wrong. She'd showed no such emotion. Mareka had watched as her low, seductive laugh had turned the heads of men and women alike.

Including Cayetano. From the way Octavia had nodded and smiled at friends and business acquaintances, as if she didn't have a care in the world, it was almost as if she hadn't vigorously rowed with Cayetano and been discarded a mere two weeks ago.

And it was also clear that the other woman was taking her cue from Cayetano. Mareka had suffered enough of those looks from her parents to recognise Octavia's a mile away—the blank look that said that, while she found Mareka inconsequential, she was still an object of intense dislike.

A combination of all her worries added to the butterflies already swarming her belly as Mareka stood frozen in front of her mirror on her wedding day, clad in a jaw-dropping lace-and-silk wedding gown.

Telling herself that things would all change once she was married didn't matter. Hell, it sounded borderline desperate, because she'd spent far too much time wondering if Cayetano *would* change his mind. Whether his coldness stemmed from cold feet. She hated herself for dwelling on it, and hated that she couldn't dismiss the cold churning in her belly.

That jitteriness made her jump at the knock on her door. Her head snapped up as her Tahitian mother entered. She'd chosen a sleeveless, saffron-coloured gown with an arched collar that highlighted her dark-gold skin to perfection, the faint grey hairs at her temples swept up into the mass of corkscrew curls Mareka had inherited. A matching saffron-coloured clutch bag, satin heels and the small but tasteful teardrop diamonds her husband had given her for her fiftieth birthday five years ago completed the look.

Their eyes met in the mirror. She wanted to tell her mother she looked beautiful but the thought of inviting the disdain she'd just been lamenting stopped her.

'This isn't a sentimental mother-daughter talk, if that's what you're afraid of,' her mother said coolly once the make-up artists and couturiers had made themselves scarce.

Mareka wondered if that was what her mother feared. But she had enough butterflies swarming her belly; she didn't need any more by asking. 'Then what it is?'

'That…fiancé of yours is quite charismatic.'

'Is he?'

Her mother sent her a droll look, then brushed invisible lint from her dress. 'Your father and I merely wanted to say, if you feel out of her depth, it's not too late to pull out.'

Alarm knotted in Mareka's throat. 'Thank you for your concern, Mother. But I'm going to marry him.'

The firmness in her voice was new to both of them. Her mother's eyes flared the tiniest bit, then faint colour flared across her cheeks. 'Well, if you insist on going ahead, don't say we didn't warn you.'

The knot melted to acid, threatening to choke her. It took several swallows for Mareka to speak clearly. 'Is that what you're really worried about? Or are you more worried that I'll embarrass you somehow?'

Another flash of surprise, then the customary disdain. But Mareka felt the faintest triumph for standing up for herself. For not being lessened on such a crucial day. Before her mother could confirm anything, she hurried to end it. 'I really need to finish getting ready. Thank you, Mother.'

Still she lingered, as if she wanted to say more.

It was a relief when a brisk knock interrupted her. 'Come in,' Mareka called out, desperate for a saviour.

When that saviour turned out to be the man she'd promised to wed, she couldn't halt her gasp.

'Caye... Cayetano.' She wasn't quite used to calling her boss and soon-to-be husband by his first name, at least not out loud, and especially not when he'd reverted to being a remote stranger these past two weeks. Every time she did, she felt a little jolt in her midriff. Telling herself she had a right now, that he'd all but commanded her to use his first name, didn't stop the waves of shock from travelling through her system as he prowled into the room.

Or was it because, simply put, he looked criminally breath-taking in his morning suit? It really should be a chargeable offence—on top of all his other lofty accomplishments—to look this magnificent.

His hair was slicked back, the sunlight slanting through

her French windows catching on his angled cheekbones and jaw, outlining the thick, sensual curve of his lower lip.

'Everything all right, Mrs Dixon?' The question was aimed at her mother but Caye's assessing eyes were pinned on Mareka.

'Of course. I was just leaving.' She hesitated, her gaze darting between Caye and Mareka.

Mareka barely registered when her mother left the room, her focus so absorbed in Cayetano.

'Traditionally, I'm guessing this is where I gasp and protest that you're not supposed to see me until I walk up the aisle?' Her attempt at humour emerged with cringing doses of nerves and breathlessness.

Had he come to tell her he'd changed his mind, finally? That, like her mother had suggested, he found her unsuitable after all?

He shrugged thick shoulders that would have drawn envy from a rugby player and kept coming, not stopping until he was within arm's reach. 'You could, but it'll just waste time. We both know what this marriage is.'

A clinical and emotionally devoid vacuum. 'So, was there something you wanted?' The question was low, tremulous, far too reflective of her inner agitation. But she supposed, if he was going to tell her the wedding was off, it was better done here, in private, rather than out there where the eyes of nine hundred guests would gleefully judge her for her inadequacies.

'I saw your mother entering your suite. I noticed at our dinner the other night that you two don't seem to have the…warmest of relationships.'

Mareka was highly disturbed by the relief that swarmed her. Just as she was both ashamed that he'd noticed the frostiness between her parents and her and astonished that he'd been moved to check on her—pleasingly so, she alarmingly admitted to herself. 'So this is a… You just came to see if I was okay?' she pressed, despite her relief. For some urgent reason, she needed to be sure.

One brow rose. 'Just?' His gaze lingered on her face, then conducted a slow, thorough survey over her body. 'A wellness check on my future bride minutes before we're married isn't a trivial thing,' he delivered, sending peculiar sensations on a whirlwind tour through her belly.

When those incisive eyes rose to rest on the pulse hammering at her throat, she swallowed. 'So you haven't changed your mind?' she blurted before she could rethink the wisdom of it.

If he hadn't been as close as he was just then, she wouldn't have seen the tiniest jolt move through him. Narrowed eyes drilled into her. 'Is there any reason why you would think I'd change my mind?' he asked, his voice low, charged…*suspicious*

'Mareka…' His voice held something heavy—a warning, maybe.

Peering closer at him, she was stunned to see the expression in his eyes. Not quite panic—men like Cayetano Figueroa didn't panic about anything—but it was a faint facsimile of it, heavily overlaid with warning.

For some reason, Mareka wanted to laugh, because it was a relief to see that tiniest chink in his formidable armour. That he wasn't completely as conceited and indifferent enough to believe he only needed to click his fingers for everyone to fall into line. Maybe she'd overblown his chilliness these past two weeks.

It lent her much-needed strength to lift her chin and look him straight in the eye. 'No. I haven't changed my mind. It'll take more than a five-minute conversation with my mother to do that.'

The flicker disappeared, replaced now by curiosity. Something she wasn't about to satisfy since she'd given away way more than she'd intended. 'And, now that's settled, shall we get on with it? I'm sure your guests don't want to wait for ever.'

'They'll wait as long as I want them to,' he said dismissively, his eyes still boring into hers. Then, just when she thought he'd leave, he did the opposite and stepped closer.

Her breath hitched. 'What…what are you doing?'

'Something else I think we need to get out of the way,' he murmured. She knew exactly what he meant because her pulse was leaping, the blood thundering through her veins. And those incredible eyes were now on her lips.

'Caye…'

'Hmm, that's exactly how I want you to respond, that's exactly how I want you to look when we repeat this out there in front of everyone. *Si?*'

Before she could answer, he cupped her cheeks, propelling her body into the heated column of his.

She was too shocked to move, possibly too *afraid* to move, just in case he stopped whatever it was he planned to do. Because the blood rushing through her veins, the faint roaring in her ears and the racing of her heartbeat screamed that she wanted to find out.

Perhaps it was because of the dispiriting encounter with her mother, or even the detached front he'd displayed in the past two weeks that had battered her, that made her pliable. She willingly curved into his warm body as he pulled her closer. As foolish as it was, she wanted a new experience to dispel this constant feeling of inadequacy that cloaked her.

It made her move into his body, arms rising to circle his neck almost of their own accord, welcoming his tight, masculine moan as his lips sealed hers for the first time.

She knew she shouldn't be doing this but, even as the argument rose, it died away, the sweep of his tongue wreaking magic, making her moan in turn.

Their first kiss should have been at the altar. A formal brush of lips, held long enough to fool everyone present. *This* was far more than that. This was the kind of magic that could make a mockery of everything she needed to hold at bay. And yet she couldn't have stopped it if she'd tried.

Because she had fantasised about this; had wondered what he would taste like, whether it would compare to anything she had experienced before. To her mild dismay, it didn't—not even close. It was heaven and, a few desperate seconds later, it was hell—because, now she knew, she feared that nothing else would compare. This kiss would stay with her for ever, canonised as the ultimate example of what a kiss should be.

It was this disturbing little thought that made her take a hasty step back far too late, trying to pull herself out of the wreckage before she was completely annihilated.

'W-what was that for?'

One eyebrow rose even as his tongue slid over his bottom lip, as if still wanting to taste her. And, of course, that sent another surge of heat through her. She wanted to tell him to stop doing that, to stop delivering mixed signals that assaulted her emotions, but her heart wouldn't communicate the plea to her lips.

He gave a slow, lazy shrug. 'I needed to be sure.'

'About what?'

'You think I haven't noticed that every time I've

touched you, you either jolted or startled like a frightened little bird? I couldn't have that at the altar.'

She lifted her hand, again the movement outside of her will, and touched her lips.

So, this had all been a test.

Mareka wasn't sure whether she hated him or envied the clinical, strategic focus of his every deed. But she hated that he could be rational in moments like these when her senses were flailing all over the place.

She turned away, hoping to hide her dismay. 'I suppose you now have your answer.'

He shrugged. 'Perhaps a deeper moan will work better, and if you feel inclined to cling to me for a little longer we might just pass muster.'

Despair grew colder, engulfing her whole body. Still, she managed to nod. 'I'll bear that in mind. Now, if you're quite finished, should we get on with this?'

Her brisk tone drew narrowed eyes, a flash of irritation passing over his face before he nodded. 'Indeed. I will see you at the altar.'

His sharp gaze lingered a few more seconds, as if gauging the veracity of her response. Again, she saw that flash of vulnerability cross his face. It shouldn't have melted the knot of desolation, or even loosened it a little, but by the time his imposing form disappeared through the doorway her emotions had turned a full one hundred and eighty degrees.

And, for good or ill, her emotions were shrouded by the memory of that kiss. As the designers and co-ordinators returned to the room and bustled around her with the last-minute touches, she dwelled within that bubble, all the way outside to where her father waited, his face a neutral mask, hiding his disdain as he held out his arm.

As the minutes passed, she welcomed that little haze. It kept her from freaking out when she walked downstairs, stepped out onto the lawn and saw the sea of faces staring back at her. Besides her mother and father, not a single relative was present. She'd wanted it that way, unable to face adding the scrutiny of curious family members of this marriage of convenience.

Inside that little bubble, she held her head high, dismissing whispered conversations and lingering gazes on her dress and diamonds.

Not that she would have been able to concentrate on them for long. Because, at the head of the aisle, his eyes fixed squarely on her, waited Cayetano. His gaze propelled her forward, her father forgotten beside her. It was only when his eyes darted sideways, with a brisk nod to her father, that she summoned a smile before her gaze was recaptured by Cayetano.

Everyone else ceased to exist the moment he held out his hand to her. She knew what this was—she accepted deep down in her bones it could be nothing else. They'd made an agreement and she was here to fulfil it.

Yet somewhere in her heart lurked the excited little illusion that just wouldn't quieten down. The chirpy little voice that dismissed the nature of this endeavour and simply revelled in the fact that she was wearing a gorgeous wedding gown, holding on to the man who'd taken hold of her secret little fantasies for far too many months.

And when she faced him, their audience now significantly quieter and more attentive, she couldn't help but look into his eyes. Did she care that he looked as solemn and grounded now as the first night he'd put this in motion? Her heart didn't. She followed the celebrant's direction, locked eyes with the man whose ring she would wear for the next three years and repeated vows that should've been clinical and emotionless, but instead resonated deep within her until they touched a special place that should've been secret. Even so, she couldn't dismiss the little nugget that, for good or ill, she was living out a secret yearning.

Giving a little mental shrug, she allowed the bubble to linger, to swell just that smallest bit. After Caye's deep, even tones repeated his own vows, they were pronounced husband and wife.

A dart of alarm struck her when he pulled her close, his warm hands wrapping around her shoulders, eyes steady on hers. She knew what was coming. They'd already had a practice run, after all, so she didn't flinch or gasp when Cayetano's lips lowered to hers.

What she did feel was that resurgence of electricity, right from the bottom of her toes to her hairline, from the base of her spine to the pulse racing at her throat. And, because she was growing shamefully addicted to that feeling, she slid her arms up his chest, resting them on his shoulders as he kissed her, murmuring growing around them as he lingered, and lingered, drawing whispers and coughs from their audience.

When he released her, he held her for a moment longer, for which she was thankful. Because her senses were swimming, her eyes blinking in the sunlight as her pulse frantically raced away.

As a ruse, it was perfect, the blushing bride dizzy from her new husband's kiss. From the smug look in his eyes before he turned them both to face their guests, she knew she'd come through with flying colours.

Mareka couldn't help herself. She basked in that approval for the next few hours, accepting congratulations and air kisses from people she didn't know and would probably never meet again.

Even her parents, enjoying glasses of vintage champagne served in eye-wateringly expensive crystal glasses, were just a touch less severe and disapproving, the esteemed guest list seeming to impress them.

As speeches were given—including one by Cayetano in absurdly magnificent tones, drawing equal parts humour and the kind of swoony indulgence that made romantics sigh—she continued to exist in that bubble, ignoring the older couple who'd been abruptly introduced at a gala a few days ago by Caye as his parents.

She told herself it didn't matter that they stared at her with heavy censure and deep scepticism. Her laughter came easily from within the bubble, their first dance a flight across a dance floor that could've been made of clouds.

So, yes, it was entirely bone-jarring when she was brought back down to earth hard, the bubble bursting with soul-shrivelling devastation.

CHAPTER SIX

THE RECEPTION WAS in full swing, guests spilling out all over the estate blissed out on good food, vintage champagne and excellent company. There was nowhere Mareka looked where she didn't see a contented cluster of guests.

Cayetano had opened his home completely to his guests and, boy, were they taking advantage of it. So, the search for her new husband, the man who had slipped the exquisite platinum wedding band onto her finger—a ring, she'd discovered, commissioned from Smythe's as part of an extensive collection—took a little longer than she'd expected.

Mareka went from group to group, pausing to laugh and allow herself to be teased that she'd lost her husband so soon after her nuptials. Slowly, though, the teasing stopped being amusing, the ominous tingling at her nape rising to mock her.

She noticed the hand clutching her barely touched glass of champagne was shaking, due to her stretched nerves, and gave a half-hearted snort under her breath. Her thought screeched to a halt, along with her feet, when she heard the loud voices coming from Cayetano's study. The room was in shadow except for the beam of late-afternoon sunlight slanting down onto father, mother and son.

Their body language spoke volumes.

She should know. From the age she'd begun to be able to read body language, she'd deciphered her parents' with unerring accuracy. She knew when a simple glance from her mother, or the way her father angled his body, meant Mareka shouldn't speak or approach but remain seated or supply a specific answer to a specific question posed by a dinner guest.

Right now, Cayetano stood opposite his parents, his shoulders frozen in formidable challenge. And, while rage bristled from him, Mareka spotted that same faint fracture she'd caught earlier.

'You choose today to confront me with this?' he demanded.

His father shrugged. 'You hardly take our calls any more. This was an opportunity we couldn't pass up.'

Caye's jaw clenched. 'I don't take your calls because, just like everyone else, you only contact me when you need something—namely money.'

Mareka's heart squeezed, despite the acid in his voice, then she flinched as his father laughed. It was an echo of a sound she'd heard from Cayetano before.

'Surely you're not still hung up on the sentimentality of your youth? You're your own man now, as you're so eager to laud over us. And you should be thankful—we were responsible for your single-mindedness. It's time to show some gratitude.'

Cayetano's fists bunched, even as a bleak shadow darkened his face. 'Or what? Let me guess, you think you have some leverage over me?'

His parents exchanged a smug look that curdled Mareka's blood.

'We know this marriage of yours is a sham. And, yes,

we want a place on the board in return for not causing ripples in the company. Or are you going to claim you've fallen in love with the gold-digging little nobody?'

For a tense moment, Cayetano remained silent. Mareka feared the blood rushing through her ears would prevent her hearing his response but it did not. She heard it loud and clear.

'No, I don't love her, and I may barely even know her. But unlike you, Father, I don't plan on letting capricious emotions stand in the way of securing my birthright. And you forget, if you do anything to jeopardise this company, you will suffer the repercussions too.'

She should've walked away then and somehow found a quiet place to stitch the torn emotions his words had caused back together. But that bleakness wouldn't let her. She knew too well the anguish of having uncaring parents. And that tiny link of affinity propelled her through the doors.

To confront three sets of eyes that held varying expressions. But it was Cayetano's she sought.

'Are… Is everything okay?' she asked, then her breath caught when she saw the cold rejection on Cayetano's face.

His father's glinted with mockery and malice. 'Ah, the fake bride come to rescue her beloved, *si*? Save your outrage, girl. We know all this is one big façade.'

'You will address my wife with respect,' Cayetano warned icily.

His father's brow arched but he didn't reply. Perhaps sensing he was treading on dangerous ground, he remained silent.

It was his mother who spoke. 'Call us next week. We expect a place on the board by the end of the month. And don't even think about slithering away from this, son.

We can make claiming your precious birthright harder than you think.'

Cayetano's nostrils pinched white, his mouth settling into a thin, formidable line. But he kept silent. And, after another mocking glance at Mareka, his parents left.

Mareka's insides continued to shake like a leaf. She sensed Cayetano coming closer but she couldn't bring herself to look at him, chiefly because she feared exposing her pain to him.

'Mareka, are you…?'

'You want them to speak to me with respect? Where is yours?' she spat out.

His eyes narrowed to slits. 'Excuse me?'

Shut up. Don't say it!

But her lips were already moving, her anguish demanding an outlet. 'You told them you don't love me, that you don't even know me.'

That I'm a little nobody.

His face clenched tight. 'And which part of that was untrue?'

Her insides shrivelled, because of course he was right. The only thing wrong with this situation was that she'd fooled herself into existing in that bubble for too long.

'I thought it didn't need to be spelled out, Mareka, but perhaps it does. So, before this goes further, you should know that it'll be a mistake to develop feelings for me.'

That shrivelling intensified. Still, she managed to raise her chin. 'You really think incredibly highly of yourself, don't you?'

His chin went up sharply, then he exhaled. 'As long as we understand each other.'

'Don't worry. I know exactly where I stand.' She turned

away, desperate to find that quiet place now. Desperate to address that tightness in her chest.

'Oh, and Mareka?'

Her feet stalled, dread stiffening her limbs. 'Yes?'

'In future, don't feel the need to rush in to defend me. I've been dealing with characters like my parents my whole life. I'm quite adept at it. Perhaps you should try dealing with your own parents,' he delivered with a dark, distinct edge.

That final spear of hard truth killed the last of her fantasy. The hard diamond cutting into her flesh told her she'd closed her thumb over it. But, as much as it hurt, it grounded her. 'You don't need my help. Got it.'

She fled to the nearest bathroom. Shutting the door behind her, Mareka blinked hard and fast, desperate not to the let the building tears overflow. When she failed and a few drops fell, she swiped at them, a half-exasperated sob leaving her throat.

She would *absolutely* not cry over this. Because she didn't care what Cayetano thought of her. *Right?* She was in this solely because she'd felt a tiny bit responsible for his plans falling apart. That stupid crush was well and truly behind her, and she could finally stop believing there was any affinity between them. *Right?*

When the affirmations failed to rush forward to her defence, she gritted her teeth, a terrible little eddy of panic making her insides dip and dive before she clenched her belly. She swiped at her cheeks again, thankful when no further tears fell.

Dragging in a breath, Mareka checked her reflection in the mirror. Mercifully, the damage wasn't too awful. A quick tissue repair and she looked almost good as new.

Lifting her chin, she turned away from the wisps of desolation in her eyes and strode to the door.

The past fifteen minutes had been more than enlightening. Cayetano's past had hardened him against all feeling. Against anything that would hold him back from achieving the only thing that mattered to him—his precious Figueroa Industries.

He'd married a woman he felt little regard for to achieve his aims. Mareka needed to emblazon that fact on her heart and mind, even if it left a cold, hollow ache inside her.

She thanked her stars when the reception started winding down less than an hour after the unfortunate incident in the study.

But, even in that short time, it was hard to avoid Cayetano's piercing scrutiny. She managed it, barely, by making sure she always talking to someone else when she sensed he was about to address her.

Her grandmother had often commended Mareka on her stoicism, but had then added that she lamented that stoicism was sadly finite.

Mareka felt that finiteness dwindling every time Cayetano slanted his green-eyed gaze at her, his imposing personality attempting to prod her into acknowledging his presence. Perhaps even into simpering, the way she had the past two weeks?

Recalling how accommodating she'd been made her stomach churn, even as her chin lifted higher, the fervent need not to be cowed burning through her until she feared she would alight with it. Until the champagne flute trembled in her hand.

Mareka sensed more than saw Cayetano's gaze on her

shaking hand. 'Careful, *querida*,' he murmured. 'Your emotions are showing.' His tone thick was with warning.

She couldn't help the grating laughter that erupted. 'And we can't have that, can we?' she retorted, sharper than she'd intended.

A few guests sent them furtive glances, sensing a delicious plot twist in the air. Mareka wasn't at all surprised when a strong arm circled her waist, the hand resting on her hip delivering a warning all on its own.

'It's time to whisk my beloved wife away, I believe,' he said to the nearest guests. 'I think I've shared her with you all for long enough.'

Good-humoured ribbing and laughter followed and within a minute applause heralded their definitive exit.

She allowed him to guide her across the room, his easy smile belying the tension rippling through his body. It wasn't until they were outside on the terrace that she spotted the helicopter at the end of the lavish landscaped garden, its rotors slowly picking up speed.

She remembered then that somewhere on the endless itinerary was an item she'd paid very little attention to: *honeymoon in Cordoba.*

Her feet dragged, her senses spinning as she kicked herself for not paying more attention to it. Her hesitancy drew Cayetano's attention. His own feet slowed, then he stopped altogether. Before she could act, he was drawing her close. Mareka opened her mouth, desperate indignation burning another path through her.

'Before you say something you might regret, remember we still have an audience,' he warned silkily. 'We've come this far, *mi esposa*. Let's not ruin everything now, *si*?' The back of his fingers drifted down her cheeks as he issued the warning.

But she was on the last of her reserves of stoicism. 'What would you care about not ruining anything?'

He leaned in, brushed the tip of his nose over hers and, on the pretext of mimicking a kiss, he breathed, 'I'm moments away from shutting you up as the only way I know how to salvage whatever is causing this riot within you.'

She gasped. 'You have a nerve. If you don't want to concern myself about your feelings, that's fine. But don't you dare demand that I turn mine on and off like a tap. Besides, you've got what you wanted now. I think I've fulfilled my part, don't you?'

His eyes flared just that small fraction, then it narrowed before his gaze dashed to the left. The action drew her own gaze. Her pulse leapt when she saw that their guests had indeed gathered on the terrace high above the garden and were watching them.

And, almost in the same space of awareness, she felt Caye's hands reposition over her body. One hand drifted down her arm and over her waist to hold her still. The fingers caressing her cheek only moments ago slid to her nape, curling warmly and solidly to hold her still.

Without warning, he bent her backwards in a romantic dip that made the terrace erupt with applause. Then he did the thing he'd threatened and sealed her mouth with his. The riot he'd mocked just moments ago erupted inside her but it was created entirely by the feel of his mouth moving over hers, not the righteous anguish blazing in her heart.

And, yes, Mareka hated herself for every second she allowed him to toy with her for the sake of their audience. Every second she secretly relished his touch when she should've pushed him away.

Dizzy when he pulled away, her response was pure self-preservation. 'What next? You're going to get on your knees and remove my garter with your teeth?' she threw out tartly.

'I would if you were wearing one.'

'How do you know I'm not?'

A strange light glinted in his eyes. 'Because I pay attention, *querida*. To everything.'

'Is that supposed to scare me or reassure me? Because, I'll tell you now, it's doing neither.'

'Then I'll have to work harder, won't I?'

'This is funny to you, isn't it?'

'What are we talking about, exactly?'

'Are you serious? Did you hear what I said two minutes ago?'

He grimaced. 'All I see is an overwrought bride.'

'An overwrought bride you don't care one jot about, isn't that right?' she whispered, those sharp spikes digging deeper.

Another gleam came in those hypnotising eyes. 'Why, dear wife, I don't remember us agreeing to *care* for one another.'

The breath strangled in her lungs and once again her heartbeat thudded in her ears. 'You're right. I'm being a fool. But I didn't think you'd be so surprisingly cruel.'

He stiffened, then his eyes shadowed. And once again she was stunned by the mercurial emotions swirling in the eyes of the man she'd only recently thought was an unbreakable enigma.

Cayetano straightened, still holding her firmly in his arms. Ignoring their audience, he swung her into his arms and strode for the helicopter.

Just before they boarded, he lowered his lips to her ear. 'Perhaps learning that this early is for the best, *querida*. Now neither of us will be disappointed.'

* * *

The words ricocheted in her head for the fifty minutes they were transported to another of Cayetano's lavish residences, this one in Cordoba.

Perhaps it was her emotional agitation, or the fact that she'd already become numb by the sheer scale of Cayetano's wealth, that her stunning surroundings failed to move her.

The sun had just set but remnants of fading light shone over the light stone building, casting it in a golden glow. But all Mareka could concentrate on were the fingers wrapped around hers despite their lack of audience as he led her into the villa in which they would be spending the next week.

She'd discarded the train to her dress after the ceremony, the clever design having transformed it from ceremonial dress into an elegant ball gown that enabled her to move freely. So, when she yanked her hand free the moment they stepped into the opulent living room, she could move away unhindered, her glare warning him to stay away as she wrapped her arms around her middle.

Cayetano eyed her for a moment, then sighed. 'This wasn't quite how I envisaged our first evening as man and wife going.'

She scoffed. 'Do me a favour and stop trying to act the beleaguered husband. As you said yourself, outside of an audience you don't really care about my feelings.' She glanced around, the need to put more distance between them growing more imperative by the second. She needed to before any more of those traitorous tears betrayed her again. 'Is there a housekeeper around, or should I just pick the first room with a bed in it?'

He didn't reply, just watched her in that intense way

that made her fear he could see deep beneath her skin. Right into the heart of her, in fact.

Unable and unwilling to withstand it, she rushed towards the door. He stepped into her path before she was even halfway across the room.

'I will allow disagreement. What I won't allow is prolonged friction.'

'That's funny, I don't seem to recall that being a specific requirement in our contract.' She threw out a halting hand when he opened his mouth. 'You seem to think you control me, Cayetano. That I'll let you treat me however you want. You may think I'm some low trash, but I won't take insults from you.'

He frowned. 'I don't think lowly of you.'

Anger snapped at the leash holding her temper tightly. 'Really? I didn't exactly hear you leap to my defence when your father called me a little Miss Nobody.'

His jaw tightened. She was sure he wasn't done, but she was.

Weariness sapped at her physically and emotionally. Suddenly, every strenuous second of the past two weeks rushed at her, draining her of energy. 'I've fulfilled my end of the bargain. So just let me be.'

He watched her for an uncomfortable stretch. Then, as if accurately guessing that he wouldn't get anything more from her, Cayetano nodded.

As if summoned by his employer's will alone, the living room doors opened and a short, middle-aged butler walked in. With a few words exchanged between his employer and him, the older man, expression as neutral as a blank canvas, bowed and ushered Mareka out.

She didn't bother to say goodnight to her husband.

He had proved conclusively that she was just a cog

in the wheel of his greater plans. Beyond that, she was as inconsequential to Cayetano Figueroa as she was to her parents.

CHAPTER SEVEN

CAYETANO SHUT THE double doors to his private suite behind him, barely suppressing the urge to slam it. Leaning against it, he dragged his hands down his face.

Everything had gone off-kilter, it seemed, from the moment this morning he'd spotted his now mother-in-law lurking in the hallway outside Mareka's room and had felt it imperative to find out what she was up to.

No, scratch that. He knew exactly when the derailment had started—when he'd invited his parents to his wedding. That had been his first mistake. True to form, they'd attempted to manipulate him the first chance they'd got.

He shook his head, despising the swell of bitterness in his gut that they couldn't even pretend to be happy for him, even if that happiness was not really genuine. That they'd mocked him for that brief display of emotion…

And then there'd been Mareka's parents. He'd been stunned that such cold, uncaring creatures could have produced a woman who tried not to but inevitably wore her heart on her sleeve. A woman who'd somehow made being out of her depth in the lofty and cutthroat echelons of Buenos Aires society a fascinating spectacle he'd been increasingly absorbed in observing.

As for the way he'd lashed out at her…

He replayed the conversation in his study, teeth clenched as it unfolded. He could blame his parents and the turbulent emotions they inevitably dragged out of him. *Dios mio*, was this what he'd been reduced to—blaming his flawed parents for his inability to control his own bitterness and disappointment?

He jerked his head back against the door, raising his eyes to the ceiling. 'Thanks for nothing, old man,' he muttered under his breath. 'I hope you're happy, wherever you are.'

He shoved himself off the door, absolutely determined not to be driven insane by this emotional circus he couldn't seem to escape. But, even as he crossed the room to the drinks cabinet, shards of guilt pierced him.

Had he been too harsh with her?

Yes, came the hissed inner voice. He'd gone too far, taken out as frustrations on the wrong person.

But the unwanted well of sympathy in her eyes, as if she knew what he was suffering… *She had no right.*

He snapped open the top button of his suddenly restrictive shirt. But, even after it was loose, shackles of shame knotted his shoulders, Mareka's pained expression flashing in his mind's eye.

He sat down for barely a second before he was upright again, pacing his private living room to disperse feelings he wasn't used to. Feelings that had curiously developed shoots since that night back in London two weeks ago, when the idea of marrying his British PA had first popped into his head.

He could stay on his lofty perch, safe in his conviction that he'd done nothing wrong—that his righteous pique was well-earned. Or he could ensure that this marriage of convenience didn't start off on the wrong foot.

He had enough experience with letting things fester to know that it wasn't a good idea. Hell, hadn't he been apprehensive about her going through with this sham marriage in the first place? The last thing he wanted was to push her into doing something foolish such as triggering the fault clause in their agreement.

Grim-jawed, he headed out of the door again. Urgency gripped him, but that too he tossed on the pile of insane incidents he didn't want to fully acknowledge, never mind dissect.

In under a minute, he was rapping on her door. Seconds felt like hours as he waited, sweat beading the edges of his temple as he waited for her to answer. When she did, she opened the door a mere crack, her dull gaze dragging slowly up from his feet, taking her time, as if she couldn't stand to look at his face.

He wanted to be annoyed with her, but a different tingling took hold of him—as had happened far too often when this woman looked at him with expressive eyes, the effect of which he suspected she had little inkling.

'Come to rub more salt into the wound?' Her voice was stiff, a little shaky, and a whole lot affronted.

Caye opened his mouth, but the words rehearsed on his way over dried up. He shook his head. 'Not quite. Invite me in.'

Raised eyebrows questioned his audacity and promised more fire. And again there was that stirring in his blood. The urge that had driven him to explore her body, to kiss her not only before they'd been married but afterwards, on the lawn, when the compulsion had grown too fierce to resist as she'd stared him down.

'Why would I want to do that?'

He took a half-step closer, glorying in the escalated

pulse racing at her throat. 'It's our wedding night,' he replied because, damn it, something about her made him a little crazy. 'Some would say it's practically a crime not to spend at least some of the night together.'

Her eyes widened a fraction, then narrowed, flashing vicious warning. 'I don't know what you're playing at but it's been a long day. I'd like to get to bed, so please just say what you came to say. Then you *will* be leaving,' she insisted.

Leaning against the doorjamb only delivered him a deeper sample of her alluring scent. That off-kilter feeling sharpened. 'I may have been a little harsh earlier,' he confessed.

'May?' she challenged, a beautifully shaped eyebrow arched.

He pressed his lips together. 'I'd really rather not have this conversation with a door between us.' A door she clung to. Examining her closer, Caye got the faint sense that he was missing something. Was she paler than she'd been before?

'Really? This Little Miss Nobody got the impression the conversation was over.'

Damn. As he'd suspected, that slur had pierced the deepest. He debated walking away, but this strain would be there in the morning, and Cayetano didn't want that. Inhaling sharply, he did something he'd never done before—he dipped into his past.

'My father has an unfortunate habit of zeroing in on the things he thinks I care about and…destroying them,' he bit out, jerking upright when she winced and paled further.

'What do you mean?'

'It means that jumping to your defence in that moment would've only made his attacks more vicious.'

'So you let him insult me…to spare me?' Her voice brimmed with scepticism.

'You heard most of our conversation. Do they strike you as people who wouldn't sink to such a level?' he quipped, bitterness searing every word.

Again, something soft and accommodating filled her eyes. He hated himself—and, yes, perhaps her—for the powerful urge to grasp it; wrap it around himself. 'No, I suppose not,' she murmured, then winced.

Cayetano frowned. 'What's wrong?'

She shook her head. 'I… It's noth—'

'It's clearly something,' he cut her off. 'The quicker you tell me, the quicker you'll be able to get rid of me.' The same compulsion had him pushing the door as he spoke, his breath expelling harshly as he saw the state of her hand. '*Dios mio*, what did you do?'

She flinched at his harsh question—something else he'd have to apologise for later. Dropping onto his haunches, he brushed his fingers over hers in silent enquiry. When she flexed her fingers, he examined the two-inch cut slanting across her wrist. Digging his free hand into his pocket, he wrapped the handkerchief over the bleeding cut. 'How did this happen?'

'A series of hilarious mishaps worthy of a comedy skit,' she said, although the visible pain on her face made a mockery of that explanation.

He had to forcibly loosen his clenched jaw. 'I'm not laughing, Mareka. Why the hell would you not mention it when I knocked?' Another question was why he was so unnerved by the sight of her in pain. Since he didn't care for the answer, he rose and, for the second time today, he swept his wife into his arms.

'You're really going to have to stop doing that, you know.'

'Why? Are you going to stop me?' He headed for the bathroom, only to stop in the doorway when he saw the broken glass on the floor. Carefully navigating the minor carnage, he set her down at the wide vanity table. 'Stay.'

As he turned away, he saw her roll her eyes.

Despite the unfamiliar stress turning his gut into mincemeat, his mouth twitched as he went to fetch the first-aid box. On his return, he spotted her wedding dress crumpled in one corner of the bathroom. Until then, Cayetano hadn't fully registered what she was wearing. He looked now and one of the many knots in his gut surged into his throat.

The white lace teddy clung like a second skin beneath the thin layer of her silk robe, the ties of which were loose enough to show her body from neck to thighs. The combination of lace, an abundance of tumbling dark-gold hair and her skin, having gained a deeper glow since her arrival in Buenos Aires, made his fingers tingle with the need to touch. Hunger such as he didn't remember plagued him, urging him to explore.

'Are you just going to stand there with the kit while I bleed to death?'

Dios mio, the way she spoke to him! He tried to recall when he'd been foolish enough to believe her timid or unremarkable.

He bit back a growl when he saw the bloodstains on the sleeve of her gown. Flicking on the tap, he held her hand beneath the cool flow to wash off the worst of the blood, his temperature rising when her pulse jumped beneath his fingers. 'You still haven't told me what happened,' he bit out gruffly. Too many disturbing scenarios darted through his brain and he particularly hated the one taunting him that perhaps he was the reason she was hurt.

Santo cielo. Surely not? He looked up in time to catch the perplexed look on her face. 'What?'

'You looked almost…ill there for a moment. You're not squeamish at the sight of blood, are you?'

Cayetano took her furled hand in his, ignoring the increased tingle in his own. 'I'm not.' Gently coaxing open her hands, he surveyed the damage, then exhaled in minor relief. The cut wasn't deep. Dousing a cotton bud in antiseptic, he warned, 'This is going to sting. Perhaps it'll take your mind off it if you tell me what I want to know.'

She sighed and, when her soft breath brushed his jaw, Cayetano stiffened his body. It was that or lean in and ask her to do it again.

'It's not really a big deal. I was trying to get out of my wedding dress; I underestimated how much effort went into securing me into the thing. I knocked the vase off the vanity and cut myself when I reached for it.' Her hand jerked in his as the astringent liquid touched the wound.

'Tranquilo… Lo siento…' he murmured, abstractedly registering that he was gentling her in Spanish and that it worked. Her shoulders relaxed and she released the bottom lip she'd drawn between her teeth. He finished cleaning her hand and reached for the bandage. His hands obeyed his command to move gently, quickly, efficiently. But, everywhere else in his body, Cayetano couldn't control his reaction to her scent in his nostrils or the smoothness of her thighs. To those plump lips she kept gnawing.

Por el amor de Dios, why was his body insisting on behaving as if he were an untried schoolboy? 'You could've called for help.' There was that treacherous bite in his voice gain. He wasn't at all surprised when she responded with a glare.

'From whom? Your butler?'

The taunt was deliberate. She'd had no intention of asking Cayetano for help, and the thought of his middle-aged butler putting his hands on his wife… 'No, most definitely not Manuel.'

'Well, then.' She shrugged, dislodging one sleeve of her gown.

Hunger invaded harder, drawing his gaze to that expanse of silky-smooth skin where her neck and shoulder met. Perhaps he was weak or stressed, or knew when to face the challenge, but he allowed his gaze to roam where it wanted, to devour the way his hands, his mouth and his body wanted to.

And, when her breathing grew erratic, he revelled in it because, *Dios*, it felt good not to writhe through this hell alone. From the corner of his eye, he saw her slick her tongue over her lips once more and he focused there, the action an unwanted reminder that their last kiss had nowhere near satisfied him.

'Stop doing that!' Mareka regretted her outburst the moment it left her lips.

She'd so hoped to stay calm and collected, but he made it so hard. Between the shock of his appearance at her door, the flash of alarm across his face when he'd seen her hand, the gentleness of his tending and the soft, soothing words in Spanish, she was toast.

Hell, he'd even skated close to the outer rim of a reasonable apology for his earlier behaviour—one that had plucked at her disloyal heartstrings. But the sum of it had brought her to this point, the strain of holding back this rampant draw to him driving her out of her mind.

Almost resigned, she watched his eyebrows draw high, the merest hint of amusement twitching his sensual lips.

'I'm dying to know what cardinal sin I'm being accused of this time.'

She huffed out a breath. 'You know what you're doing. The staring at my face and my mouth.' She stopped and inhaled, willing calm. Then she exhaled in exasperation as he did the very thing she'd accused him of. 'It's…it's…'

'Turning you on?' he drawled, his voice low, gruff.

And, heaven help her, there was no point denying it. The evidence was right there, her body betraying her without mercy. She wasn't even sure who moved first, but somehow her thighs had widened and Cayetano had slotted his lean hips between them. All she had to do was lean forward so she could…she could…

She jerked back, not caring that she didn't get very far, the mirror at her back stopping her. 'Yes! Look, it's distracting, okay? We're not in public. You don't need to pretend you find me attractive. I'm… I'm fine now. You can go.'

He did the opposite, closing the gap between them. 'You think I don't find you attractive?' he challenged. His warm breath brushed her earlobe, creating a cascade of shivers over her skin. 'You think I'm not rock-hard right now, imagining the many ways I can get you naked and beneath me on that bed behind me?'

Her breath was snatched clean out of her lungs, his evocative, erotic words skyrocketing her pulse. 'W-what? No…'

His lips quirked but any trace of humour was scorched from the heat in his eyes. 'You seem shocked, *querida*. Why is that?'

Mareka shook her head. 'Because I'm not a fool. Because I'm not your type…'

His finger slid over her mouth, hushing her. She shook

her head, halfway between irritated and intrigued, one of the many new states he could fling her into as easily as flicking on a light switch.

'Right here, right now, you're the only woman I see. The only woman I want.'

Words some other woman might have yearned to hear. Except…they were woefully *transient*, the unspoken implication that she was replaceable echoing desolately in her brain. She shook her head again, more for clarity than for anything else.

He sucked in a breath as her movement slid his finger over her lips…her *parted* lips.

Before she could stop herself, or debate the wisdom of her action, her tongue slid out, flicking over his warm flesh.

Another sharp intake of breath and he wrapped his whole hand over her jaw, cupped her nape and brought her close. 'There's the fire I crave.'

'You don't…crave me. You can't.'

He laughed wickedly and low, and so erotically her pelvis melted as heat flooded her. 'Is that a challenge?' he whispered, those mesmerising lips hovering dangerously close. 'Shall I prove to you just how wrong you are, *guapa*?'

The 'yes' her soul wanted to eject thankfully stayed trapped in her chest. Neon signs blazed that this was the height of foolishness, and yet the essential 'no' also remained jammed in her throat. 'This is insane,' she finally managed, even as her fingers twitched towards his lean waist, so tantalising close. It would be so easy to grab and hang onto him.

His face spasmed, then that small, enigmatic smile flashed. 'That we can both agree on.'

'It's been an…interesting few weeks.'

'Indeed, and perhaps we're being handed the tools to deal with it.'

The devilish coaxing in his words caused the melting sensation to intensify. But she strove to hang onto her resolve. Anything else would be catastrophic. 'You don't belong to me.' The fractured words were torn from deep inside, from a place she didn't want to examine. And, just because they made her feel oh, so vulnerable, she tossed in a defiant, 'And I don't belong to you.'

'Also true,' he said. 'But we can lend ourselves to each other just for this night. Just until the insanity passes, no?'

Until the insanity passes…

It was both a highly dangerous but excruciatingly seductive offer. As he'd suggested just now, the moment would be finite, but this time not in a way that would wrench her to pieces, because this would be purely physical…a carnal, mutually satisfying episode….wouldn't it?

What was he even suggesting—a kiss? A make-out session up to a point, then withdrawal? What if she couldn't hold herself back?

Firm fingers speared through her hair, his grip directing her to meet his gaze.

'You're over-thinking this,' he purred, his voice low and thick with need.

Her hands twitched again, then almost of their own volition rose to rest on her thighs, tantalisingly close but not completing the journey to touching him. 'Am I? Because I'm one hundred percent sure this wasn't what we agreed.'

His nostrils flared. 'Maybe not. But we thought we could resist this unstoppable need to have each other two weeks ago. Had I known it was impossible, I would've ensured it was very much in the small print.'

She tried to shake her head, but the formidable man planted in front of her didn't give her a chance, his grip tightening in a way that was deplorably erotic, need arrowing straight between her legs. Her nipples hardened, her blood heating and finally, *finally*, her thighs closed around him, tangling her legs with his.

His grunt was part-need, part-encouragement, all arrogant smugness. His gaze dropped to her heaving chest and the hard points of her arousal, his breath hissing out again, the barely tamed bulge behind his fly flexing with his need.

'You want me,' he declared in that same self-assured tone. Eyes fixed firmly on hers, he added, 'You want this.'

Heaven help her, she did. But one last spurt of rebellion wouldn't allow Mareka to surrender—not just yet. But she could tap into the sensation he'd stoked so effortlessly between them. So with a jagged moan, she surged forward, meeting the sensual lips already bearing down on hers.

Heat, desire and pure sensation flared high, driving them even closer. When Cayetano's tongue swiped over her lips, demanding entry, she freely gave it, starved for this act that felt as imperative as her next breath. He groaned when their tongues clashed, decadently tasting her with bold, hungry licks that drove up her insanity. Wanton, agitated breaths escaped them as they strained for more sensation and devoured what was offered.

He broke the kiss, his breathing harsh as his forehead rested on hers. 'Touch me.'

It was a gruff order, wrapped in savage need. She realised that, through all this, her hands had stayed off his body: perhaps she could take a modicum of satisfaction that a tiny fraction of her was safe. She finally raised her hands and slid them around his waist to pull him even closer.

His groan of encouragement spurred her into exploring the tight, packed muscles of his torso, trailing one hand up and over his chest before her nails dug into his nape, whimpering as her lips searched his for another kiss.

'*Si*. Just like that,' he encouraged.

Was she really doing this—throwing caution to the wind so soon?

It's your wedding night.

It was unconventional, and not at all what she'd envisaged for herself the few times she'd allowed her thoughts to drift into the future, but...

She'd already stepped way out of her comfort zone. What was one more step? The neon sign flashed brighter. But the taste of him, the feel of him... Mareka shuddered as Caye cupped her breast, his thumb torturing the sensitised peak. Heat pooled between her thighs, unfurling fresh need through her.

It was good, unlike anything she'd experienced before, which was why she whimpered again when he broke the kiss and drew back. 'Tell me you want me, *guapa*,' he ordered thickly.

'Yes,' she muttered.

Her greedy, roaming hand wandered below his belt and, in one uncommon move driven by need, she cupped his rigid length, gasping when she felt the power and girth of him.

'*Dios mio!* Not here. I need to see you, feel you properly.'

With that, he plucked her off the vanity table. Her legs tightened around him, bringing her heated centre into direct, searing contact with his steel-hard arousal. Her moan collided with his hiss, and she watched him squeeze his eyes shut for a moment before that molten gaze was directed on her once more.

The crunch of glass beneath his feet as he walked them out of the bathroom sparked a reminder of how they'd ended up there. But it was engulfed by bigger, more demanding flames. So, when her robe slithered off her shoulders in the trip between her bathroom and his bedroom, Mareka let it fall free. And, when Cayetano laid her across his bed, with her clad only in the lace teddy she'd worn for her wedding in a moment of 'why the hell not?', she let those flames move through her, destroying the layers of diffidence and disquiet she'd felt since the study incident.

She allowed her arms to land above her head, heart surging into her body when Cayetano paused as he straightened. He remained braced over her, one hand on the bed and the other on the third button of his shirt, and simply watched her…with fierce focus…with visible arousal…with *hunger*.

For someone who lived in a world where she was either an afterthought or totally forgotten, this was…stirringly *addictive*.

His gaze seared down her body, lingering at the vee of her thighs. 'Knees up.'

She didn't immediately comply. She yearned to see his reaction, to watch that hunger build along with his impatience. The very few occasions she'd seen Cayetano's patience fray had been eye-opening. It was a risky road to take, yes, but she wanted more of it. So she waited until his eyes darkened further, her thighs sliding together as she returned his stare.

'Seems like you're in the mood for dangerous games,' he said.

'Maybe.'

He reared upright and disposed of his shirt. The first sight of Cayetano's bare chest, and the packed muscles overlayed by golden skin, was intoxicating. Powerful enough to make her jerk her knees up, ready to give him what he wanted.

Sensual lips quirked as his hand went to his belt, her re-action fuelling his smugness. She might lose this thrilling little game but not without scoring a point or two. Arch-ing her back, Mareka let her thighs fall open.

Cayetano sucked in a harsh breath, his fingers fum-bling with his fly. A moment later, he abandoned undress-ing altogether to grasp her knees. Nudging them open, he stared at the heart of her covered with the thin layer of lace and muttered thickly in Spanish. The thrill intensi-fied, making her moan, making her restless.

Without warning, Cayetano, the most powerful man she knew, dropped to his knees. But his power was in no way diminished. And he demonstrated it by dragging her body to the edge of the bed, his gaze on fire as he hooked the flimsy material aside, lowered his head and delivered a private kiss that yanked a scream from her throat.

'Oh! Oh, God!' She could barely breathe, her hands dropping down to grip his thick shoulders as her senses dove into free fall.

Green eyes hooked on hers over the undulation of her body, once again delivering that rabid scrutiny that elec-trified the magic he was delivering. 'Is it good, *guapa*?' he drawled.

Her fingers convulsed on his skin, digging in. 'You know it is.'

He lifted his head a fraction and laughed, low and wickedly. 'Why does that sound like another accusation?'

His mouth continued to wreck her even as he carried on the conversation and, for another deliciously puzzling reaction, it sent her closer to the edge. An edge he pushed her off with the next series of flicks of his tongue that made her scream. She came down from the best high of her life to find him braced over her, she a specimen once again pinned beneath his fierce regard.

'You were saying?'

'D-don't pretend you don't know. You're s-smug and arrogant because you're clever at everything!'

Shadows chased fleetingly across his face. 'At this, perhaps. But not quite everything.'

'Show me, then,' she challenged and, in the tense seconds that followed, wondered why she was pushing this, pushing him, after everything he'd said to her tonight and after she'd discovered just how easily he could wound her. For reasons she couldn't pin down, she didn't repel this man. Hell, she would go as far as to say she had the opposite effect on him. Even now, those eyes were fixed on her as if he couldn't look away. So why not press home her advantage, study him just as he seemed intent on studying her? 'Just one flaw.'

His nostrils flared. 'And why would I do that?'

'Just so I know you're human.' So she knew that the touch of vulnerability she'd glimpsed earlier hadn't been an aberration.

He contemplated her for a long stretch. She held her breath, the need to see beneath the formidable exterior clamouring. The need to learn what made him tick, what made him scared and what made him *happy*.

Mareka realised she wanted to know his *heart*.

Oh, God.

'Does this not feel incredibly human to you?' he enquired, his voice gruff, sexy and far too mind-wrecking.

Her eyes flew open. Before she could voice the question, he breached her heated core, surging into her with a forceful thrust that punched screaming pleasure from her throat.

'Answer me, wife,' he ground out against her ear.

'Yes! Oh, yes.' She lifted her hips as she gasped the words, meeting him halfway as he plunged back inside her.

It made him hiss. 'Ah, *si*. More of that.'

'Only if…if you do that again,' she returned.

Despite the strained control on his face, his teeth flashed in a feral grin. 'Even in this you fight and resist.' He pulled back and thrust deep again. 'Is this what you want?'

'Yes!' She gasped, pleasure tearing through her. 'Please. More!'

'*Si. Mucho más…*' He breathed other hot, sexy words against her heated skin but she was too far gone, too steeped in bliss, to make them out. All she knew was that he more than delivered, each penetration driving her towards a peak she both feared and embraced.

At some point she realised he was doing that thing again—watching her, absorbing her every reaction, perhaps even feeding off it. But this time, far from unnerving her, she revelled in it, tossing her head with feminine abandon, spiking her fingers through his hair until he hissed and groaned. Then she offered up her lips, whispering in a voice she barely recognised as her own, 'Kiss me.'

He did, and she met him lick for lick, stroke for stroke. Fanning the flames of desire so high, she knew she would either be born again on the other side or there'd be nothing left when he was done with her. Either way, she leapt off the peak and into bliss with a scream dragged from her soul. Ecstasy wrung her out but, even as Mareka slipped into the sweet oblivion of sleep, she feared those roots had found fertile ground.

That they were even now digging deeper into her heart.

He needed to get some sleep. To rest and rise with clarity and a fresh perspective on everything that had happened.

But Cayetano wasn't ready to be rid of her—not yet. Even now, his body stirred as he breathed the scent of alluring woman and sex and watched her sleep, wondering yet again just what it was that fascinated him about Mareka Dixon. No—Mareka *Figueroa*.

His gaze shifted from the lush fan of her eyelashes to the pulse thudding steadily at her throat, pausing at her plump, full breasts—shifting restlessly when his body stirred harder to life—before dropping to the rings on her finger.

The primal satisfaction that swelled through him at that very powerful evidence of their union was yet another puzzle he was sure would be resolved with sleep and distance. And he would strive for that distance. Nothing else would be acceptable because he absolutely didn't intend to go down the route his parents had.

He'd effectively distracted Mareka from probing deeper, of course. Revealing what others had dared to call his emotional deficiencies—and he labelled necessary safeguards—hadn't been part of his agenda tonight. Nor would it ever be. He'd already skated too close to losing control during that exchange with his parents.

Already, feelings were beginning to seep into the equation—feelings, disagreements, the need to placate—

all of which had led them here, to her bed. At least the outcome hadn't been entirely disagreeable. They'd found mutual satisfaction, perhaps smoothed what had threatened to be a bumpy start to their convenient agreement.

Was he already attempting to justify himself? His disgruntled snort made her stir. For the first time in his life, he found himself holding his breath, not wanting to wake a woman and start the tedious process of disposing of her.

Instead, once she'd settled back against him, one smooth leg sliding over his in a way that made him bite back a groan, he brushed a whispered kiss across her temple.

Two hours later, when he still lay awake, fighting sleep, Cayetano forced himself to admit that the madness hadn't quite worn off yet. That this woman intrigued him far more than he'd been prepared to accept. Her defiance, her fearlessness—hell, even the way she didn't shy away from confronting him when he allowed his strong will and hard-earned ruthlessness to dictate his actions—was provocative. He hadn't been this intrigued in a long time. So maybe he shouldn't be in a rush to put this new…entanglement behind him.

He stared down at her, watched her eyelids flutter, then kissed them, gratified and not even a little bit regretful when she roused, blinking for a few seconds before her gaze flew to his.

'I woke you.'

Her gaze dropped to his mouth, then lower, her breathing growing rushed and beautifully agitated when she saw his erection. 'You did.' She breathed, her voice sexily husky. 'I'm guessing that was deliberate?'

He laughed, zeroing in on the target that commanded

his interest—her mouth. '*Si, querida*. And I'm not even a little bit sorry.'

Once more, Cayetano promised himself sternly. Once more, then he would be done.

CHAPTER EIGHT

SHE INTERRUPTED THEIR heated kiss, tried to push him onto his back and failed. Cayetano pulled back to meet wide eyes sparking with fire.

He smiled. 'What is it? You want to be in control?'

A nervous bite of her lip, contradicting that siren-like display she'd tormented him with earlier, was followed by a jerky nod, her lashes dropping for a self-conscious moment before her gaze met his once more.

Heaven above, but even that abashed look made him hard. With brisk efficiency, he rolled them over and settled her over his lap. She moaned at his staff nudging her core, bold in its demand. Jaw tight, he drew his arms up, sliding them beneath the pillow, fully aware of how his flexing body held her mesmerised. Morning would come soon enough and with it the imperative clarity he sought. But he fully intended to enjoy the hours between now and when sanity returned.

'It's your show, *tesoro*. What are you waiting for?'

Mareka flushed at the daring challenge, knowing he was watching her every move. That dual sensation shivered through her again: she'd gone to sleep on a blissful cloud and woken to a dangerous, addictive paradise in the form of the breath-taking specimen of man whose last name she now shared.

The sane course of action would be to draw a line under the heady experience and retreat to her own bed. Instead, she dragged demanding nails down his chest, her insides twisting in delight when his jaw clenched in a visible, intoxicating fight for control.

She rolled her hips, curbing a smile when he hissed and dropped a thick curse. 'You owe me an answer, I think,' she said, unaware the words were coming until they spilled out. She held her breath as his eyes narrowed and his fingers dug into her thighs.

'How very wily you are, to believe you've got me under your mercy.'

'Have I not?' Who was this woman, speaking these words, playing the siren when in her few previous encounters she'd been painfully inhibited, relieved when the experience was over?

'Is this your flaw, then—impatience bordering on desperation?'

A hard smile mocked that observation. 'A little desperation isn't a vice. It reminds us that we're striving for something important—essential, even. I wouldn't call that a flaw but a challenge to reach that goal and satisfy what drives us.'

'I don't think you strike anyone as a man who's ever satisfied.'

'There's a reason sharks don't stop swimming, *querida*.'

The faintest warning in those words chilled her spine. 'So, you plan to live for ever on the edge of desperation, chasing the next goal?'

He gave a rich shrug. 'It's been a success so far, has it not? Why change a winning formula?'

She shook her head and pressed forward. 'In business, maybe. But I'm not interested in that. I'm interested in what feeds your soul—drives Cayetano, the man.'

His jaw clenched. Shadows rolled over his face, reminding her of the exchange she'd witnessed in the study—reminding her that, while he seemed wholly satisfied with his lot, part of him wasn't entirely invulnerable. And, as foolish as it was, that part called to her.

'You'll find there's little distinction between the two. I am what I am, *guapa*. Don't go searching for something that isn't there.'

The warning, like the one he'd issued before, was weighted. It hovered between them, threatening to cool the heat. But even that wasn't enough to dissolve the deep curiosity stirring inside her. She opened her mouth to... push for more? To tell him he should reconsider because... what...there was more to life than wealth and financial excellence?

What did she know? Her dream was still unrealised. What if the fulfilment she envisaged didn't materialise once she'd made it come true? What if in the end she still remained second best, still someone's afterthought? What if...?

The questions and her thoughts careened to a halt when he brushed his thumb over the tight bundle of nerves between her thighs. She gasped, her fingers digging into the tight muscles of his pecs.

'Your window for taking control is fast closing, *mi esposa*. Take it now or lose it,' he warned.

A firmer rotation over her clitoris by him and she was shuddering, no longer cold or distracted. Her head fell back, her skin tightening as pleasure stretched over her.

Clearly, he was done waiting for her. Done indulging

her attempts to probe beneath his surface. And, as sensation climbed, it was easier to pretend there wasn't a hollow opening in her chest, that his rebuffing didn't hold echoes of her own past rejections.

It was easier still to rise onto her knees, grasp his rigid length where it throbbed ready and impatient between her thighs and impale herself upon it, her delighted cry drowning out his thick groan as pleasure suffused them.

She might have been on top, but Cayetano mastered her from underneath until she was a screaming mess, her throat raw from the sheer bliss of it.

The smell of coffee woke Mareka, but it was gut-churning panic that jerked her upright in bed. She glanced around, unsure whether to be relieved or disturbed that Cayetano wasn't in bed with her.

Catching sight of the beside clock, she guessed one possible reason why she was alone—it was approaching ten a.m.! Warily edging to the side of the bed, she stood up on wobbly feet, the enormity of last night's events unnerving her.

She'd slept with Cayetano—her boss, her husband, on paper—after having insisted on that very same paper that she wouldn't. Did that mean their agreement was now void?

And the things she'd demanded from him! What on earth had come over her? The sassy siren from last night had faded away in the morning light, leaving her very chagrined at her behaviour. Chagrined, panicked and blushingly sore in a way that left no doubt how sexually enthusiastic she'd been last night.

Sore and without a stitch to wear, because while she'd been in slumber-land the flimsy underwear that would've been a better covering than nothing had disappeared, along with Cayetano's discarded clothes.

She ventured towards the room she hoped was the bathroom. It turned out to be a dressing room larger than her whole London flat, with row upon row of impeccable bespoke suits and shirts lining one side and neatly stacked casual clothes on the other. But it lacked what she needed—a towel or a dressing gown to cover her body with.

Cringing at the thought of parading out naked—totally out of the question—Mareka grabbed the nearest shirt, white, long-sleeved, in cotton so rich and soft it felt like silk. Knowing it had caressed Cayetano's body at some point heightened the electricity zipping through her body as she emerged from the dressing room.

To find the man in question striding in from his terrace. He froze at the sight of her but his eyes didn't. Despite the slight edge in the green depths, they conducted a thorough examination of her body, lingering on her exposed legs and his shirt before meeting hers. 'You're awake.'

Heat rushed into her face, recalling the last time he'd spoken similar words to her and what had come after—pleasure like she'd never known before. Even now the reminder pulsed between her legs, her heart beginning that wild, anticipatory hammer.

'You should've woken me earlier,' she said, self-consciousness climbing when her voice emerged hoarse and husky, another reminder of how she'd over-used it last night.

'Hmm, perhaps,' he murmured, walking closer, then stopped two arm-lengths away.

Confusion mingled with disappointment inside her. He'd left her in bed and now he was hesitating to come close. She hadn't intended this to go beyond one night, of course, but paradoxically the realisation that he wanted the same thing bruised that vulnerable place inside her.

Enough.

Her handful of experiences had never included morning-after awkwardness, thank goodness. But she would get through this. And, yes, she told herself she was relieved when he took a step back and turned away after another tense scrutiny of her face and body.

'Breakfast is waiting. Come.'

The pressure on her bladder stopped her from following him.

He paused, one eyebrow raised.

'Um…where's the bathroom?'

He nudged his chin forward. 'Through there. Come out to the terrace when you're done.'

She nodded and hurried away.

When she was done, she lingered before the mirror, holding her wrists under the cold tap in the hope that it would calm the roiling inside her. Mareka noticed that she couldn't quite meet her own gaze, couldn't comfortably confront the woman with sex-tousled hair and reddened, swollen lips after the first shocked glance.

But, knowing she couldn't stay in the bathroom, she sighed, turned off the tap and headed back out. Halfway across the vast bedroom, she heard him. The conversation was tense, delivered in brisk Spanish. It shouldn't have made her already knotted stomach tighten even more, but it did, the reminder that she was being quickly relegated to second-best the morning after her wedding striking deep.

Her steps faltered at the terrace doorway as she accepted what was happening to her—she was jealous.

Searingly, blisteringly jealous of Cayetano's first love—his company.

It was a low feeling but one she couldn't help any more than as she could stop breathing. Taking a deep, stabilising breath, and vowing to deal with this unwanted feeling, she forced her feet to move.

The sight of Cayetano's tense, bare upper body exposed to the worshipping sun as he cradled the phone next to his ear, his other hand deep in his pocket, made her hesitate. The hard stone that wedged in her chest made it hard to breathe as she watched him turn and heard him bark something into the phone before he hung up. She watched him saunter over to where she stood, that neon sign she'd ignored mocking her with its brilliance.

His eyes narrowed and, once again, he stayed out of arm's reach.

When she couldn't stand that unnerving scrutiny any longer, she raised her chin. 'What? You're staring.'

His face hardened, and his eyes flicked over her shoulder in the direction of the very rumpled bed. 'You woke up in a bed you willingly slept in, *querida*. Therefore, there should be no wrong side to grumble about.'

Heat and irritation twisted inside her. 'Excuse me?'

He didn't answer immediately. He turned and walked towards the corner of the sun-splashed terrace, where a pristinely laid table held a sumptuous breakfast. When he reached it, he pulled out a chair, rested his hand on the back of it then quirked an eyebrow at her. 'Clearly, you're discontented about something. I'm speculating that it's not because you woke up on the wrong side of *my* bed.'

Mareka frowned.

She'd never thought she was a tightly closed book, but she hadn't imagined she was that easy to read either. But evidently one of Caye's many talents included a direct line to her thoughts because, the moment her traitorous gaze darted to the phone in his hand, his own features morphed from edgily neutral to hard, cynical amusement.

'Ah, I see.' He waved her to the seat and, lips pursed, she approached and sat down. Only to exhale sharply when he leaned forward and murmured in her ear, 'And this is where the proverbial claws and ultimatums come out, *si*?'

She tensed. 'I have no idea what you're talking about.'

He tossed the phone on the table, took his seat, reached for a cafetière and poured her coffee as if he didn't have a care in the world. Perhaps he didn't. After all, it was just *her* feelings in the way. And he'd warned her that he didn't deal with feelings, hadn't he? 'I'm assuming that my words are coming back to bite me in the butt,' he commented, nudging milk towards her.

'Cayetano, I don't—'

He held up his hand, and she bit back an unladylike curse. 'I was the one to…encourage a minor alteration in our agreement. And now you feel the door is open to make other demands, yes?' His even tone was in sharp contrast to the cynical disappointment reflected in his eyes.

The gall of him. Forcing herself to meet those incisive eyes, she aimed what she hoped was a carefree smile his way. 'I see why a man who lives and breathes for the next blood-stirring negotiation might feel that way. But you can rest easy that, in my case, you couldn't be more wrong if you tried.'

The flare of surprise was quickly doused by cynicism and narrowed-eyed suspicion. 'I'm extremely well-versed in the act of feinting, Mareka. I think we've established by now that I don't play games.'

'Neither do I. You think I'm about to make lofty demands just because we've slept together.' Praying he wouldn't see how her body eagerly reacted to the recollection, she continued, 'Be reassured that I don't want anything from you beyond what we agreed before we got married. Hell, I'll go as far as to encourage you to forget that last night happened at all. We can carry on as we'd intended to.'

He remained deathly still during her rambling. Now a muscle ticked in his jaw, a forbidding glint turning his eyes hauntingly beautiful...and extremely dangerous.

'You're serious.'

'Why wouldn't I be?' she parried, then let out a light laugh, which thankfully didn't sound as strained as it felt leaving her throat. 'Look, I'm sure you're used to women fawning over you the morning after and pleading with you for repeat performances. Thankfully, for both our sakes, I'm not one of those—'

His ringing phone interrupted her. Mareka clenched her jaw. 'Aren't you going to get that?'

His own jaw tightened. 'No.'

She looked away and took her time serving herself some scrambled eggs, a buttery croissant and a small bowl of fruit, painfully aware he was watching her the whole time. 'Don't stop yourself on my account.'

Displeasure pulsed from him, his lips thinning. Then, in a lightning-fast motion, he stabbed the reject button and tossed the phone away.

'Why did you do that?' she enquired coolly, forking a piece of melon and popping it into her mouth.

'Because I don't wish to speak to my grasping, conniving parents. Especially not today. And also, because we're in the middle of a discussion.'

Oh, yes, the edge was back in his voice. Had they been discussing anything other than last night or the unsettling subject of parental relationships, Mareka would've been amused. As it was, she was playing the role of a lifetime, pretending to be blasé about the most memorable night of her life.

'Are we? Oh. I thought we were done.' She tossed in a moue of irritation and watched his chest rise in a slow inhale.

'No, *mi esposa*. You had just finished expressing how last night was no big deal to you. Except, unfortunately for you, I know different. Your inexperience gives you away.'

She almost choked swallowing the melon. And, *damn him*, his lips quirked just before he poured a glass of water and set it down in front of her. Mareka didn't touch it. And she didn't glare, despite yearning to do so. 'I beg your pardon?'

'Even without the benefit of having you in my bed last night, I knew beforehand you've only had two notable relationships.'

'How...? You had a report done on me?'

'Are you surprised? Weren't you lauding my business acumen only a short while ago?'

'But that...that was...'

He raised an eyebrow when she stumbled to a halt. 'Yes?'

Her appetite fast withering away, Mareka set down her fork. 'I can be inexperienced and still not care to repeat what happened last night,' she felt compelled to insist.

Her breath shuddered through her lungs, her heart leaping in betrayal at how much it wanted that to happen.

I don't love her... I may barely even know her... I don't

plan on letting capricious emotions stand in the way of securing my birthright...

She repeated those harsh words to herself, knowing that, no matter how tempting repeating last night might be, she valued her self-worth more than that.

'You wanted me last night. You still do. It would be no trouble at all to refresh your memory.'

Mareka swallowed, the unshakeable certainty in his voice intensely disarming. She shook her head. 'A refresher won't be necessary.'

'Why not? Because you still feel me inside you, *guapa*?' he enquired so silkily, she felt the intoxicating effect echo through her as if he was touching her.

Her fingers curled around the edge of the table. 'Have you stopped to consider that not letting this...brief entanglement...happen again might be as good for you as it is for me?' His amusement evaporated but she pressed ahead. 'What was it you said—that I shouldn't make the mistake of developing feelings for you?'

She attempted a laugh again, and silently fist-pumped when she pulled it off once more. 'You're totally off-base, of course. But, since you seem to think you're entirely irresistible, why would you want to risk even a mild infatuation when you can chalk this up as the event it was?'

'And what label is it to be slotted under?'

'Wedding night madness? An itch scratched? We're both adults. We don't even need to define it as one thing or another.'

His lips thinned and he glanced off over the terrace for several seconds before refocusing on her. 'Do you really mean that? Or is that a placeholder statement until you're ready to admit your true feelings on the issue?' he taunted.

Recognising that she was nearing the peak of her performance of nonchalance, that she risked her composure crumbling, she rose and set her folded napkin primly on the table, disregarding the fact that she was wearing a shirt...*his* shirt...and nothing else. 'Yes, Cayetano, I really mean that.'

Fortunately, his phone began to ring again. Frustration gleamed aggressively in his eyes.

'You should answer your parents. Or it is business? I guess you didn't send the memo that you're on your honeymoon?'

'As one of my PAs, you know perfectly well that my business doesn't have set hours. My temporary marital status was never going to change that.'

The reminder of the impermanent nature of their pact hit home hard, even as the phone continued to shrill. 'Great, then I'll leave you to discuss your business.'

She headed for the French doors, praying she made it out in one piece. The slight hitch in her step came when he pushed back his chair, ostensibly to attend to his neglected phone.

Mareka told herself she was relieved when he barked out an irritated, *'Si?'* a moment later.

But, long after she'd returned to the sanctuary of her room, had taken off his shirt and entered a bathroom swept clean of broken glass—long after she'd scrubbed herself clean of last night's debauchery, hoping it would lessen the searing memory of it—that knot remained hard, unsettling and taunting her with its vibrant existence.

From her new, breathtakingly gorgeous wardrobe, she selected a light, halter-neck maxi dress. The sleeveless, backless design left her arms and back cool...and, no, she didn't choose the moss-green colour because it reminded her of Cayetano's eyes. She'd merely learned to dress for the hot climate.

Tying her hair in a loose ponytail, she rubbed sun-protection lotion over her exposed limbs and face, then finished with a slide of colourless lip gloss.

Then, seeing Cayetano's shirt on her bed, she snatched it up. She couldn't exactly wipe her memory clean of what she'd done last night, but the last thing she needed was a visible reminder.

But she hesitated as she neared Caye's suite. Would it be better just to hand it over to one of the maids? God, how hopeless was she if she couldn't stop her face burning over such a simple thing? Clicking her tongue in impatience, she strode to his bedroom door, knocked, waited for a minute and then, when she didn't get a response, turned the knob. He probably wouldn't hear her if he was still out on the terrace.

The room was empty and, curiously, there were no sounds coming from the terrace. Her already unsettled emotions took a lower dive when it struck her that he might already have gone down to his study and started his work day—the day after his wedding.

Had she hoped that after their argument he'd change his mind? Change *who* he was? Shaking her head at her naivety, she headed for the dressing room, only to freeze when she sensed him behind her.

Turning, she felt her jaw sag. 'Oh, I thought...'

He froze when he saw her, his eyes darting all over her before coming to rest on her face. *'Si?'*

She tried desperately to suppress the effect of his mouth-watering body. Last night, she'd been too overwhelmed to take him in fully. Now, confronting a fully naked Cayetano, heat suffused her from head to toe.

He'd just stepped out of the bathroom, the towel riffling through his hair the only piece of clothing on his body.

When she didn't answer, his gaze dropped to the shirt clutched in her fist. 'What are you doing?' he rasped.

It took every scrap of willpower she had not to drop her gaze below his neck. 'Putting back your shirt,' she replied. Her hand gripped the expensive cotton a little too tightly, almost as if she didn't want to let it go. But she had to. It was entirely too significant a reminder that she was getting used to this. *To him.* And she couldn't afford that.

His gaze darkened, then he shook his head. 'Keep it.'

'Why? I don't need it any more.'

His nostrils flared. 'I have three-dozen more. I'd prefer not to become fixated on just this one because it's been on your body,' he said with a dry edge.

She sensed that, while he hadn't hesitated to reply, he wasn't altogether thrilled about admitting what was tantamount to a need—perhaps even a *yearning*. It was such a total, disarming reflection of what she was fighting, justifying extreme caution. So why did the thought fizz up her blood, excite her enough to send heat into her face?

The answers to that remained locked inside when he closed the space between them. One finger slotted beneath her chin, tilting her face to his gaze. 'I'm not in the mood to argue with you, *guapa*. Not when I've taken the day off just to spend it with you.'

'What?'

His mouth twisted in sardonic amusement. 'Shocking, I know.'

Her traitorous insides leapt with giddy delight, just before she slammed the lid on the wild joy. 'You didn't need to do that.'

'It's already done,' he said simply, imperiously. Then

his eyes roved over her dress. 'Although, you will need to change your delightful dress.'

'Why, what are we doing?'

'I thought we'd start in the stables and see where we end up. I have a few horses who have been missing my presence for a while. Have you ridden before?'

Was it insane that the knot shrunk just that little bit? 'I took lessons one summer a long time ago, when I was a teenager.' Her parents had made friends with a horse enthusiast and academic who'd been well-positioned to offer her father a tenured professorship. Mareka's sole job that summer had been to befriend the academic's teenage daughter.

'Then you're not a complete novice.' His gaze dropped to the shirt for several beats before he shook himself out of whatever thought had gripped him. 'Meet me downstairs in ten minutes.'

CHAPTER NINE

MAREKA TOLD HERSELF that she was going along because she'd questioned what to do with herself today. Since they were in Argentina, all work fell under Octavia Moreno's remit, and the last thing Mareka felt like doing was clashing with her.

Besides, any outside activity would be a welcome distraction for things she didn't want to think about. And if Cayetano, the consummate workaholic, had taken a day off...

Ignoring the voice teasing her for making wild excuses, she re-entered her suite and crossed to the dressing room. Relieved that her new wardrobe came with five sets of jodhpurs and matching tops, she reached for a green set, once again ignoring the mocking voice. So what if she wanted to wear green today? It was just a colour, for heaven's sake! Done with more than five minutes to spare, she snatched the shirt off the dressing room island, bundled it into a ball and stuffed it in her underwear drawer.

Out of sight and all that...

Downstairs, Mareka drifted towards the living room, returning greetings from curious staff as she went. The living room was even more stunning than she remembered. A grand fireplace over which hung an exquisite painting immediately drew the eye as the focal point. From there, two groupings of contemporary furniture and plush rugs blended comfort with tasteful opulence, the kind she'd come to associate with Cayetano.

She'd just perched on one overstuffed chair when he walked in. For a second, she was glad she was sitting down.

He looked...*magnificent*. The all-white of his riding gear was sharply contrasted by a black belt and polished black boots. The way his polo shirt emphasised the breadth of his shoulders, and the trousers his lean, athletic hips, made Mareka's mouth dry. Finger-combed damp black hair made her fingers tingle with the urge to run though the lustrous waves. She was trying to process the depressingly acute reaction of her body when he stopped in front of her.

'First things first,' he rasped.

Her heart jumped into her throat, but he only reached for her hand. Lifting it, he inspected the bandage that was still mostly in place.

'How does it feel?' he murmured.

'Oh. It's...fine. Just some mild discomfort.'

He nodded, then turned to the newly materialised butler, who held out a first-aid kit. Five minutes later, her cut was redressed with the kind of gentleness and care that left Mareka with the circumspect notion that her husband wasn't the cold, cutthroat individual he wanted projected.

A prospect that weaved deeper within her, leaving her shaky and bewildered as they stepped outside to a waiting electric buggy. Because, in letting that possibility take root, Mareka knew that guarded, vulnerable place within her that wanted someone to...*care* was softening, making way for the impossible.

'Everything okay?'

She startled. 'Of course, why do you ask?'

'Because you vowed to seize the day and yet you look positively pensive.' His gaze dropped to her hand. 'Is it your hand? I didn't hurt you, did I?' he asked sharply.

And there it was again, that increased softening. She shook her head equally sharply to dispel the frightening sensation. 'No. I'm fine.'

His gaze lingered on her for another stretch, then he aimed it at the small hill they were climbing. Cayetano's estate was vast, with groupings of buildings dotted in the distance. After travelling for about ten minutes, they arrived at a long, low wooden building, the equine smell announcing the stables before they pulled up in front of large barn-like doors.

Several stable hands greeted them with respectful smiles, their eyes lingering curiously on Mareka. An older man with salt-and-pepper hair and weathered features stepped forward and shook hands with Caye.

'This is Andrés. He's the head of my stables.'

A small smile cracked the man's face. *'Bienvenida, señora,'* he said in a raspy voice.

Shaking his hand, she returned his smile. *'Gracias.'*

That his eyes twinkled at her attempt to speak Spanish lit up a warm place in her belly. Before she could caution herself for getting too carried away with this soft, warm feeling that might come back to bite her down the road, Caye was guiding her into the stables, his hand splayed on her lower back.

She told herself they were in public, that this was what they'd agreed. Yet, she couldn't help but melt into his touch or stop her body from swaying closer to his. From the heated glance he sent her, he'd caught the betraying movement. And, as they went deeper into the stables, she couldn't help a muted gasp when his hand drifted lower, lightly cupping her backside, before it dropped away.

Her body lit up like the inside of a volcano. Blood roaring in her ears, she didn't make out what Caye said when they stopped in front of a half-door. But she got the gist of it, another gasp leaving her as she saw the creature within.

The stunning horse with a shiny, caramel-gold coat and chocolate-brown eyes, watched Mareka carefully as she approached, then nudged her the moment she reached touching distance. From somewhere, Caye produced a wedge of apple and held it out to Mareka.

The moment she was fed the treat, the mare nudged her again. 'She's the calmest in my stable. But she can also be quite demanding,' Caye said drily.

'She's beautiful. What's her name?'

'Caramelo. A little obvious, but suitable, *si*?'

It took far too much effort to look away from Caye's indulgent smile as he ran his hand down the beautiful horse's forehead. After murmuring to her for a minute, he turned to Mareka. 'Are you ready?'

She inhaled deeply. 'As I'll ever be.'

At Caye's nod, Andrés opened the door and led the mare out. Caye moved a few doors down. A minute later, he led out a black stallion, whose dark eyes surveyed them before he threw his head back in imperious outrage.

Watching the two formidable creatures was like watching a theatre play of dominance. Cayetano won, of course, mounting the saddle with smooth, masculine grace that sent a pulse of desire straight through Mareka. She strove for even a fraction of that poise when Andrés helped her onto the saddle. A three-minute refresher course—thankfully easy enough, because muscle memory kicked in—

and they were heading over another shallow hill. Two more, and the estate was spread out before them.

They rode in companionable silence for fifteen minutes before the vista was broken up by towering cypress trees.

'It's beautiful here,' Mareka murmured.

'*Si,*' he breathed. 'Sometimes I forget.'

She glanced at him, surprised at the touch of bewildered nostalgia on his face. 'Because you rarely take time off to enjoy the fruits of your labour?' And maybe it was the stunning vista, or the air seeping pleasure into her bloodstream, that pushed her to continue, 'We seem to be doing things that are outside of our norms.'

His eyes glinted in that breath-catching way. Then, his face growing taut, he shrugged. 'But I daresay we'll revert to type soon enough.'

He sounded so completely certain that it struck discordantly within her, triggering that absurd need to challenge him—yet again.

Reading her emotions, one corner of his mouth twitched. 'Are those sparks I see, *guapa*?'

She sucked in a breath and resolutely shook her head. 'No. Not at all. I've decided it's too lovely a day to spend it disagreeing with you.'

Was that disappointment dulling the glint in his eyes? His shrug a second later shattered that notion. 'A wise decision.'

He'd taken the day off.

The concept was as foreign to Cayetano as the low rumble of temper simmering beneath his skin, resistant to every attempt to dislodge it. Octavia had been equally as shocked when he'd issued the unheard-of instruction to cancel every appointment in his diary for the next twenty-four hours, leaving his opinionated and increasingly supercilious PA lost for words. He'd gone one better and instructed that Octavia herself should not contact him unless the world itself was on fire.

Knowing that not only were company matters on hold but that his parents couldn't contact him again—couldn't fill his head with harsh but ultimately empty threats that emphasised their avaricious intentions—produced a hollow relief he hadn't expected. And, no, he wasn't about to dwell on the fact that both his mother and father had forgotten what today's date meant. If he didn't talk to them, then he didn't risk betraying that, after all this time, it still seared that they'd forgotten. As they'd forgotten so many milestones in the past.

He'd taken a day off and he'd experienced a peculiar satisfaction in powering off his phone for the first time in…hell…he couldn't remember. When he'd stepped into a cold shower after that, he'd hoped it would restore sense and wash away this ache and need pounding through him, but no. Every breath searched for *her* scent; every rush of the water over his skin had triggered a yearning for *her* touch.

He'd never strayed close to dependence on anything or anyone, and yet, as he'd stepped out of his bathroom this morning, he'd feared that he'd developed a taste for his new wife that couldn't be shrugged off the morning after.

The scent of pine mixed with the smells of smoked meat from the distant *parillas* soothed him a little, but he couldn't take his eyes off the woman as comfortable on his mare as if she'd been born in the saddle. Her initial nerves had evaporated and, from the swing of her ponytail to the delicious curves of her bottom, her ease drew his eye.

Hell, *everything* seemed to draw his attention—including how she'd casually dismissed any prospect of a repeat of last night with a shocking resolve that'd unsettled Cayetano and, if he was brutally honest, bewildered him.

It wasn't because she hadn't found pleasure in his bed. She had—from the way she'd screamed her pleasure, the way her nails had dug into him, her unfettered responses and demand for satisfaction fuelling his desire like never before. *Dios*, he was getting hard just thinking about it and since when had he allowed himself to be led by his body?

He clicked his tongue and his horse increased its speed to match hers. 'Enjoying the ride?'

She blushed, and a strange, rough calm rumbled within him. Misery loving company? Desire fuelling unwise desire?

Her gaze swept down to the mare, and a punch of something absurdly resembling jealousy struck him when she smiled at her and ran a hand down her neck. 'She's a dream.'

He curbed the absurd urge to demand the same touch from her. To tell her he'd given up his day for her and therefore was entitled to satisfaction too. He bit his tongue because he wasn't a needy child. He hadn't been one since he'd recognised that he needed to grow up fast if he didn't want to be trampled on the battlefield of his self-absorbed parents' toxic marriage.

'Does the air always smell like this?' she asked.

He grasped the lifeline to suppress thoughts of his childhood and his parents. 'Like you're in an evergreen forest but with a possibility of discovering barbecue in the middle of a fiesta around every corner?'

Surprised laughter spilled from her. The sound, light and far too delightful, burrowed deep inside him, somewhere he knew he couldn't reach to discard it very quickly.

'Yes. It's fascinating. And also hell if you're hungry.'

He frowned, recalling she'd barely eaten anything before the disagreement had disrupted their breakfast. 'Are you?'

She shrugged. 'I can wait till lunch...'

Her response trailed off to nothing because, seeing a worker tending one of the many posts, Cayetano beckoned him over.

'What did you say to him?' Mareka asked when the young man had hurried off to relay Cayetano's instructions.

'Ensuring my wife doesn't go hungry.'

The colour deepened in her cheeks. 'Oh, you didn't have to do that. I would—'

'We were set to have a picnic in an hour. I'm merely bringing it forward. No big deal.'

No big deal.

For the next half-hour, Mareka wavered between being touched and fighting to seal up that vulnerable spot inside, torn between being angry and hurt that something that seemed so simple to him was gaining such significance to her. Because when had anyone cared *this* much for her comfort and wellbeing?

'Mareka?'

She jumped, then realised he'd stopped, dismounted and was staring at her while she grappled with something that was *no big deal* to him.

'Yes?'

He tossed his reins around the branch of a nearby tree before he strode towards her, loose-limbed and annoyingly breath-taking. 'I said we're stopping here.'

'Oh. Okay.'

He watched her for a moment, then raised his arms. Her heart leapt into her throat. Again. At this rate, the organ would wear itself out before she completed her first day as Mrs Cayetano Figueroa. She glanced at the ground, judging whether she could make it down on her own, because she could really do with her emotions calming down a little around him.

'You've injured yourself once,' he said wryly, accurately guessing her thoughts. 'Let's not add another injury so soon, hmm?'

Another wave of heat sweeping up her face, she pursed her lips and settled her hands on his shoulders. A smooth, effortless swing and she was on her feet in front of him.

As predicted, his scent immediately attacked her. She turned her head before she took a deeper breath, then consciously pulled away, striding over to gaze at the vista. Cayetano followed after dealing with the mare, standing far too close for her roiling senses. To distract herself, Mareka said the first thing that entered her head. 'This looks like the sort of place that stays in families for generations. Did you grow up here?'

He stiffened, then shrugged. 'On and off. This was my grandfather's primary residence. I tried to spend as much time here with him as I could when circumstances permitted.'

'Circumstances?' she probed gently. 'Are you talking about your parents?'

His profile grew even more remote. 'My parents aren't a subject I normally discuss if I can help it.' The words were clipped out, his closed-off expression discouraging further interest on the subject.

'Ah, but didn't we agree today was not a normal day?'

The eyes that met her flared with surprise despite the

hardness lingering. Then it turned to speculation. It was almost as if he was considering her response, not dismissing her out of hand.

The feeling that came with that notion was…warming. But, when the silence stretched, she started to accept that the feeling had been premature. He wasn't about to open up about what she suspected had been his turbulent childhood just because they were acting out of character.

He opened his mouth, but the gentle whine of an electric engine stopped him. Turning, she saw the young man Cayetano had sent off earlier riding towards them in a buggy. In the bed of the vehicle, a large picnic basket and accompanying accessories were stacked high. Cayetano pointed to the right, giving instructions that the man followed, turning the buggy and driving deeper into the woods.

'Come,' Cayetano said to her. 'Let's get you fed.'

That warmth returned even after she noticed that the stiffness didn't leave his face. Five minutes later, Mareka gasped in delight as they emerged into a circle of trees dissected by a wide, shallow stream. On either side of the stream, the ground was carpeted with soft grass. On the near side, their picnic was laid out on wide, soft blankets, colourful cushions tossed out in a welcoming setting that made a curious lump lodge in her throat.

It was beautiful, serene, thoughtful. And that warmth was expanding, threatening to engulf her whole heart. She jumped a little when Caye grasped her arm and led her to the blanket. She settled down on one end and he took the other. Mareka didn't mind when he chose silence, grabbing a plate and heaping it high with slices of delicious looking grilled meats, warm bread and heavenly smelling chimichurri that made her mouth water.

They ate, Caye occasionally stiffening and staring off into the distance. Mareka curbed the urge to ask him what he was thinking. It was none of her business. Besides, this had turned out to be the perfect way to spend the Sunday after her wedding, even if that wedding had been for a more clinical purpose than most people thought. She didn't want to ruin it.

'This place was my escape when things got a little too…volatile at home,' he said suddenly, disrupting the calm with the bombshell.

Mareka's heart thudded. 'Volatile? You mean…?'

He shook his head immediately. 'The volatility wasn't directed at me.' His lips twisted with a bleak bitterness that knifed through her. 'My childhood mostly involved my parents being too busy tearing chunks out of each other to be concerned with where I was on their battlefield. My grandfather was a firm believer that every marriage was meant to be, that disagreements worked themselves out eventually.' His jaw clenched once before it relaxed. 'It took him a while to realise that his son's might not be the union made in heaven he'd hoped it would be. That he couldn't even trust him to take over his company after he was gone.'

'And that the adverse effect on his grandson wasn't something he could keep ignoring?'

His head whipped towards her, his expression once again of mild surprise.

She shrugged. 'Don't look so surprised. When you're constantly on the outside of a relationship, whether it's perfect or not, you tend to notice how things should be. When it's great, you slot it into the pros column for what you want for yourself. When it's not, you know what to avoid when you have the chance. Either way, with enough exposure, you learn a few things.'

He absorbed her words for a long stretch, then his mouth tightened. 'I was well past an impressionable age when my grandfather decided that exposing me to his own union might alter my view on things.'

Mareka's heart lurched, an unknown tightness gripping her nape. 'The way you say that… It's as if…'

'He failed?'

Her nod was jerky. 'Did he?'

One corner of his mouth twisted. 'What he failed to realise was that his own marriage to my grandmother wasn't perfect either. They just learned to handle it better than my parents did.'

'That sounds uncannily like you think you know the code to a perfect marriage,' she said, attempting a lightness she didn't feel.

'Absolutely. It's to stay as far away from believing a perfect marriage is possible. Or stay away from marriage altogether.'

An icy-cold sensation froze out the last of the warmth. She was glad she'd managed to eat something before now because, just like this morning, her appetite deserted her with shocking speed. 'So, because you can't have it all, your solution is to have nothing at all?' Her voice was tight with too much emotion, causing her heart to lurch again, because she didn't care for how much his bleak conclusions affected her.

Hell, *she* didn't want to know why it bruised her so deeply. Yet she couldn't stop probing. 'And what about children? Do you plan to leave all of this to your offspring or is all that driven ambition just for self-gratification?'

His eyes blazed green fire. Apparently, she'd hit a

nerve. 'I'm lucky enough to live in a time of great scientific innovation. If I ever feel the urge to procreate, there are ingenious ways to do so without trapping myself in a marriage,' he clipped out.

Mareka sprang to her feet, the urge to get away from his emotionless outlook too strong to contain. Tense silence echoed behind her but she felt his gaze on her as she stalked to the edge of the stream.

The sun was highest in the sky, relentless heat beating down on her. On a wild whim, Mareka tugged off her riding boots. The jodhpurs were a little too tight to pull up but they were stretchy enough that she managed to yank them up to her knees. In her bare feet, she waded into the shallow water.

'Mareka, you need to be careful. The bottom can be—'

She yelped, not expecting him to be this close. Turning far too quickly, she lost her footing on slippery stones. Her arms windmilling wildly, she let out another cry as she toppled, landing with a loud splash in the stream. The water closed over her for a handful of seconds before firm, strong hands wrapped around her waist and dragged her out.

Coughing and spluttering, mostly out of embarrassment, Mareka gripped his shoulders as he walked them both to the bank. By the time he set her on her feet, they were both totally drenched. His shirt was plastered to his body, the white turning translucent to reveal the tight six-pack beneath.

Her mouth dried, her fingers convulsively digging into his shoulders to stop herself from the insane need to explore his body. In turn, his eyes grew heated as they trailed over her body.

Pushing away from him before she succumbed to insanity, Mareka stumbled back to the picnic blanket, grimacing at the discomfort of the sticky cotton. She plucked at her top for a moment then, spotting the extra blanket, she gritted her teeth and tugged it off.

The sharply inhaled breath behind snapped her attention to him. His eyes were glued to her skin, his eyes still dark with latent heat. 'Insisting that what happened last night isn't going to happen again then undressing in front of me seems especially barbaric, no?' he mused, the rough edge back in his voice. Then, with a mocking look, he yanked his own polo shirt off and tossed it away. 'Especially on my birthday.'

She gasped, her eyes going wide. 'It's your birthday?'

There was a mixture of mockery and a flash of bleakness. '*Si,*' he responded simply, his eyes fixed on her.

She examined his face, trying to read him deeper as their earlier conversation tumbled through her mind. 'When you said you didn't want to speak to your parents "especially not today" you meant…?'

'That I didn't want to engage with parents who called to make financial demands without bothering to wish their son *feliz cumpleaños*, most likely because they'd forgotten? Exactly so.'

Her feet carried her to him before she could think better of it. She stopped when she was close enough to feel his body heat, but stopped short of touching him. It was best not to. 'For what it's worth, I'm sorry.'

He stiffened for a moment, then he jerked out a nod.

Her heart dancing erratically in her chest, the melting started again as she added, 'Happy birthday, Caye.'

Green eyes darkened to almost black. '*Gracias,*' he said gruffly.

His chest heaved, reminding her just how undressed

he…they *both* were. She slid off her jodhpurs, her face heating when she felt his gaze follow her with an avidness that stole her breath. Part of her almost wished the earlier iciness was back because, as she'd learned to her cost, the warmth was dangerous and misleading to her heart.

But he was walking towards her, reaching for the blanket and unfurling it. And she drunk him in, her arousal snapping over her like a silken net, trapping her within its unbreakable confines. Her gaze lingered on the droplets of water clinging to his vibrant olive skin, her mouth watering with the urge to lick them off. She moaned as he wrapped the blanket around her, then tugged her forward until barely a foot separated them.

His gaze left her face, trailed down to her chest and the scrap of shamrock-green satin and lace covering her breasts, then lowered to the matching panties.

'You have more items to take off,' he rasped, his voice a rough rumble.

The flames engulfing her intensified but she managed to shake her head. 'I don't think…'

'They'll dry quicker if you take them off.'

Glancing down at his sodden boxers, she raised an eyebrow. With a tight, far too distracting smile, he left the blanket draped on her shoulders and whipped off his boxers.

Mareka's eyes widened at the thick, unabashed erection that sprang free. When her gaze flicked up to his, his bold dare taunted her. Lamenting how quickly he dragged her into these dangerous games, she reached behind her and unsnapped her bra clasp. It was oh, so vain to revel in his thick swallow as she tossed the wet fabric away; to thrill in the sweet ache of her beaded nipples and the thick desire unfurling through her as she dragged off her panties.

Between one breath and the other, they were clutching each other, feasting on each other as greedy lips and frantic hands chased pleasure.

When the need to catch their breaths forced them apart, Cayetano's forehead dropped to hers. 'How do you do this to me?' he rasped roughly against her lips.

'Do what?' she gasped.

'Make me forget myself so completely. So damn frequently.'

'I... Are you blaming me for the way you feel?'

His grating laugh tightened her skin. 'That would be as futile as blaming the sun for rising. I'm guessing this is a *me* problem. No, *querida*, I'm blaming myself because I haven't been able to quite work you out.'

She wasn't sure whether to be flattered or disarmed. Giving up on deciphering yet another puzzle, she boldly wrapped her hand around his rigid length, her senses leaping at his thick groan. She threw her head back when he started kissing his way down her neck and chest, gasping when he drew one nipple into his mouth.

Within a minute, she was spread out on the blanket and he was raining hot kisses on her inner thigh. Her fingers spiked into his hair as his mouth found her, but she was too impatient. She needed him in another way that wouldn't be denied.

'Caye...please. Take me.'

His head reared up, eyes smouldering delicious, dangerous fire as he dropped one last kiss on her thigh and prowled his way up her body. She held her breath as he nudged her centre, then moaned in sublime pleasure as he entered her.

It was a soul-searing kind of pleasure. The skin-to-skin sensation earth-shattering...

Wait…

Skin to skin.

She tensed, a layer of pleasure vanishing.

'What is it? What's…?' Cayetano froze mid-speech, the thought careening through her head slamming into his too.

His face morphed into a harsh mask of disbelief as he throbbed inside her. Then he pulled out, rolling away, his pallor increasing as his haunted eyes searched hers. 'Last night. We didn't…'

Mareka snatched up the discarded blanket and wrapped it tightly around herself. 'No, we didn't.'

His expression turned even more haggard. *'Dios mio…'* He breathed in stark disbelief. Then he vaulted upright, his magnificent body, now a pillar of colossal tension, striding away from her. He bit out the two words a couple more times before he whirled towards her.

'I've never done that before.' It wasn't an accusation, but it was a statement of deep disbelief and displeasure.

'I'm glad to hear it, but it doesn't take away the fact that it happened.'

His hands dragged down his face, impossibly making him look even bleaker. 'I'm healthy. You have nothing to worry about there,' he bit out.

The ice crept closer, the realisation that she'd been so careless clawing at her. 'Again, I'm glad to hear it, but that isn't the entire issue, is it?' Her insides flipped over as she said the words, stark reality rushing at her like a runaway freight train.

Agitated fingers spiked through his hair as he pierced her with those incisive eyes. 'The responsibility was more mine than yours, but I have to ask…are you on the pill?' The question was flat, devoid of inflexion. But his eyes gave him away. *Everything* hung on her answer.

Mareka swallowed, her heart thumping with the truth she had to deliver. 'I was... I am... But I missed a couple of days last week, and this morning,' she whispered.

His face tightened until she was sure he'd turned to stone. *'Dios.'*

'I wasn't expecting what happened,' she felt compelled to say. Then, something sharp and awful drilling through her chest, she added, 'We can discuss the morning-after pill if you—'

'No, I do not.' A feral growl rumbled the ground beneath her, the dark flames in his eyes warning her that subject was off the table.

And, as much as she wanted to call up her feminine outrage and challenge that raw edict, Mareka backed away from that debate because she realised, deep down, she didn't want to go down that route either. Regardless of the consequences, she would allow fate to take its course.

But, despite that visceral response, Cayetano didn't look any less bleak about the prospect that she might be...

Pregnant.

The word ricocheted through her brain, a huff of shock leaving her throat as it sunk in deeper. Beneath the blanket, her fingers brushed over her belly, stroking it before she could stop herself. Then she snatched her fingers away, the spike of growing elation frightening the hell out of her. Until she knew, until they were one hundred percent sure, she was tossing weighty emotion on an already turbulent situation.

'Look, we might be worrying about nothing,' she started, but he shook his head, his movements jerky as his fingers speared his hair once more.

'On the contrary, we can't afford not to think carefully about this. Planned or unplanned, bringing a child into the world requires an essential level of commitment.'

Her heart plummeted to her feet as she recalled their conversation only a short while ago. 'And you're not ready to provide that commitment, of course. Because this is as far from the clinical procedure you outlined for yourself some time in the distant future, right?'

Fury flashed across his face. 'Don't put words in my mouth, Mareka.'

She waited and watched him pace, his expression growing grimmer by the second. She opened her mouth to tell him not to bother finding words, that she could read his body language loud and clear.

'When will we know?' he fired at her.

Her face heated. 'My period is next week. A simple test might work if I miss it, but a blood test in a few weeks will confirm either way.'

A muscle ticked in his jaw, then he resumed pacing.

'Can you…can you put something on, please?' She might have cast aside her inhibitions minutes ago, but she wasn't quite ready to embrace the brazen nudity he so comfortably exhibited.

He sent her a speaking glance before stalking over to snatch up his boxers and shove them back on. Then his hands bunched at his sides, his head shaking in disbelief.

'What?'

A cynical little smile curled lips that wreaked sweet havoc on her less than fifteen minutes ago. 'I think my earlier point is well made.'

'What do you mean?'

There came a clench and release of his jaw. 'I mean we've barely been married for a day and look where we are.'

The sun glinted off her rings just then, as if winking in agreement. A spark of anger lit through the miasma of emotions. 'A fake marriage and a possible pregnancy you don't want with a woman you barely know or care about? Unfortunately for you, the first was your idea and the second, well, that's on both of us. As for the third…' She stopped, breathing at the fresh anguish of the reminder. Then she lifted her chin. 'If it makes you less freaked out, I'll take responsibility for this.'

'I am not *freaked out*,' he delivered through gritted teeth.

She allowed herself a small smile. 'You're making a valiant show of that from where I'm—'

'And, if there is a child, I will most definitely take responsibility.' He ploughed on as if she hadn't spoken, again with the same feral viciousness with which he'd vetoed the morning-after pill.

Somewhere deep inside a knot loosened, but Mareka refused to consider it. Not here. Not now. Because, with his words spoken, Cayetano was snatching up his remaining clothes. Mareka reached for hers too, half-relieved to see that, while they weren't completely dried, they weren't still sodden either. After wrestling herself into them, she retied her hair.

But, when she started towards her horse, Cayetano stepped in front of her. 'Leave her. She'll be collected later. You'll ride back with me.'

She blinked. 'Why?'

His jaw worked as if he didn't want to say the words. 'If you're pregnant, I don't want to risk you falling off.'

'But you said she's the gentlest, and nothing happened on the way over.'

His Adam's apple bobbed but he still shook his head. 'It's not a risk I'm prepared to take,' he stated implacably.

And so Mareka found herself seated in front of Cayetano, his solid torso, arms and thighs braced around her as they made their way back to the villa in charged silence, the journey taking twice as long as before, because it seemed Cayetano Figueroa, whether he'd ever wanted a child or not, was downright primal in protecting the child his wife of convenience might be carrying.

CHAPTER TEN

CAYETANO WAS USED to fearlessly negotiating billion-dollar deals where the wrong word or a delicate ego might mean the difference between winning or losing. He'd never flinched from those challenges and, ten times out of ten, he'd come out on top.

He was flinching now.

Every ripple of horseflesh beneath his thighs ploughed fear through his gut. He wondered why he was putting himself through this. Why hadn't he simply waited for the stable hand to turn up with the buggy to collect their picnic and exchange their horses for a different, safer form of transport?

The answer blazed through his brain. Because the need to put much-needed distance between himself and the bombshell Mareka had delivered had been *paramount*. Because he hadn't been able to contain it there on the spot, where between picnic, cloudless sky and babbling stream the world had looked deceptively idyllic. Where, even in the cold depths of his shock, he had experienced that visceral punch of emotion he'd never have believed himself capable of—*primal possessiveness of his unborn child*.

This was what came of turning off his phone and leaving it two miles away. This was what happened when he recklessly pursued desire.

Dulce cielo.

A shudder went through him as the potential conse-quences of his actions unravelled inside him. Having felt his reaction, Mareka turned and glanced at him, her hazel gaze searching his. He returned the look, probing hers in turn to see how she truly felt. She'd said words that had triggered base emotions, but had she meant them? Or had they been as empty as the childhood promises his mother used to make when she'd needed his cooperation to use him to volley shots at his father?

Mareka turned away sharply, her face pinching at what-ever she'd read on his. It didn't matter, Cayetano assured himself. Nothing mattered until they knew the truth.

Then what? What the hell did he know about being a father, never mind a good one? Only this morning, on his birthday, his own father had called to manipulate and ex-tort him. He stared at Mareka, potentially the mother of his child, at the flat belly he'd kissed on his way to expe-riencing a dangerous heaven.

Had he damned himself by voicing his hypothetical future intentions? An intention he'd expressed in the ab-stract because he'd never expected to be thrust neck deep into *this*.

His hands tightened on the reins, causing the horse to toss his head. Panic flared once more, and his arm banded Mareka's middle before he took his next breath.

'*Calma. Tranquilo,*' he muttered to the horse, while securing her body tighter to his.

She stiffened. 'I'm fine.'

The assurance bounced off him, attempted to settle, but his turbulent emotions wouldn't let it. Thankfully for them both, the villa came into view just then. He was sure she breathed a sigh of relief. But all Cayetano could compute was that there was a real chance he was staring down the barrel of fatherhood. And that there were deplorably high odds he would fail at this vital task because *he* had been failed.

They were barely indoors before Cayetano walked away from her. Mareka had expected it, of course. Yet the ache arrived, sharp and enduring, leaching the last shred of hope from her bones.

Returning to her suite, she looked around blankly, unable to fathom how much her world had turned upside down in the space of a day. This time yesterday, she'd been standing in front of the mirror, wondering what her marriage of convenience would entail.

How quickly she'd found out. With jerky movements, she undressed, tossed her damp clothes in the laundry basket and, for the second time in as many hours, stepped into the shower, washing away the effects of another eventful interaction with Cayetano.

Catching sight of herself in the mirror afterwards, she hurriedly dropped the hand that had somehow found its way back to her belly. At this rate, she'd trigger wild rumours across the tabloids before she'd established for herself whether or not she was carrying Cayetano's child.

The last two weeks had shown her just how well-known her husband was in Argentina. Mareka's own name and image had been splashed alongside his. As much as she wanted to find out one way or another, going out to buy a pregnancy kit from a pharmacy would only invite unwanted speculation.

But…she could order one online.

Grabbing her phone, Mareka paused when she saw the alert from her bank. Activating the app, she inhaled sharply at the sight of her bank balance. Somewhere between last night and this morning, Cayetano had stayed true to his word. She was now officially a millionaire. On any other day, the endless zeros would've drawn more than a little awe. And, yes, when she got over the potential mind-blowing reality she faced, she would start putting the money to the essential use she'd targeted it for.

For now, she couldn't think beyond the plot twist she'd landed herself in by giving into her desires. Groaning, she tossed the phone away, lay back on the bed, tried to slow her runaway heartbeat and to just...*think*.

No matter what happened, she wanted this baby. And not in the way her own parents had taken her arrival— she wanted hers to *love*, to *cherish*. Wanted to imbue it with so much self-esteem it would be coming out of his or her ears. Everything Mareka had been deprived of, she would triple for her child.

If there was a child. Suppressing the deep well of dismay that accompanied the possibility that she might not be pregnant, she reached for her phone. Within minutes, the test was ordered, delivery arranged for the day after she expected her period. She might well be delivering a different message to Cayetano next week. But, deep in her heart, Mareka suspected her life was about to change.

The first change happened at dinner time, when one of the many maids arrived to tell her that the *señor* was tied up so Mareka would be eating on her own. She only forced herself to eat because already her brain was twisting and turning with the need to stay healthy, considering what she could and couldn't consume, what might harm the baby. She knew she drew curious gazes from the butler and rest of the staff when she enquired what ingredients were in the food, but she couldn't be bothered by that. There *could* be a more important element in her life now.

Nevertheless, it was a relief to escape back to her suite. And, when sleep eluded her—when she spent a self-pitying ten minutes lamenting her lack of trusted friends to call or an understanding mother who could've helped her deal with the rollercoaster of emotions that whizzed through her—Mareka resolutely grabbed her laptop, propped herself up on the lounger on her terrace and went to work on the second most important thing in her life.

She worked until the sun peeked over the hills on the horizon. When a yawn caught her by surprise, she smiled, the new purpose she'd set in motion warming up a cold, anxious place in her heart.

Although she managed to sleep the moment her head touched the pillow, she was up again in four hours. Deciding she wasn't going to cower in her room, she dressed and went downstairs to find that Cayetano had left. She was about to ask the staff the humiliating question of where exactly her husband had gone when a text pinged on her phone.

Left for an unavoidable appointment. Will be back late. C

The optimistic outlook she'd woken with took a dive. Apparently, the fake honeymoon neither of them had wanted was already over. She ate then donned a stunning bikini she would never have picked out for herself in a million years, but which looked surprisingly good on her. Then, with her laptop in tow once more, Mareka spent the day by the sparkling half-Olympic-sized pool.

The various emails she'd sent last night about her charity had already gained responses, some from prominent women in Buenos Aires eager to meet with her. She didn't kid herself that her new status as Cayetano's wife had nothing to do with it, but she wasn't going to look this particular gift horse in the mouth.

After setting up meetings for the coming week, she went for a swim, grateful for the low burn in her muscles that made her tired enough to fall asleep beneath the large umbrella. When the housekeeper shook her gently awake, the sun was low in the sky. Surprised, she sat up. 'How long have I been asleep?'

The older woman smiled. 'Only a few hours, *señora*. The *señor* asked us not to disturb you but I think you need a drink, no?'

'The *señor*... How did he know I was...? Did he call?' She hated the hope in her voice.

The housekeeper nodded but Mareka saw the way she avoided her gaze. '*Si*, but only to say he would not be home for dinner.'

Was that a hint of disapproval in her voice? What did it matter? Cayetano intended to carry on as normal. The quicker she took a leaf out of his book, the better. She accepted a guava and ginger punch drink, then headed inside.

She was most definitely not going to wait up for Cayetano that night, and she didn't, or on the ten nights that followed.

On the night she heard the rev of his powerful sports car just before midnight, for some reason she fell asleep soon after, her senses absurdly calmer. And, when she went down bright and early the next morning to find Cayetano seated at the table in a smaller but no less gorgeous, sun-drenched room, she was glad of her hard-fought composure.

He was dressed in his impeccable formal attire of light-blue shirt, pinstriped trousers and dark tie, with his jacket draped over the chair next to him. The financial newspaper she usually ensured he had in London was folded next to his plate, and Mareka knew he'd already consumed everything there was to know for today in the business world. One of his many talents was speed-reading with astonishing efficiency.

His gaze snapped up at her entry, then conducted a thorough examination of her body. By the time it returned to hers, heat was rising, engulfing her.

'Are you well?' he rasped, his gaze probing.

Did he mean her or the baby she might be carrying? Despite the bolstering speeches she'd given herself, echoes of past hurts hollowed her out. Sucking in a breath, she attempted to suppress the ache. 'Yes. I'm fine.'

His weighted gaze assessed her for another minute before he rose and pulled out her chair. Murmuring her thanks, she sat and sipped at some orange juice while the butler placed a perfectly made, mouth-watering omelette in front of her. Apparently her appetite had returned in full force because she devoured it in record time, much to the satisfaction of the man watching her with hawk-like focus.

Mareka decided she wasn't going to read anything into it. Cayetano's single-minded focus would remain unsettling for ever, whether she was carrying his child or not. Starting as she meant to go on, she cleared her throat. 'We never clarified my professional role while our marriage is in place.'

He stiffened, his eyes piercing hers. 'As my wife, you

have the right to any available position you want within my company. But I'll leave the decision to you.'

She took a breath, hesitated then said the words that left a hollow of loss inside her, despite knowing deep down she was doing the right thing. 'In that case, I'm officially resigning as your PA.'

A flash of surprise was quickly erased by displeasure. 'To do what, exactly? You're not going to work for someone else,' he stated with a steel-edged voice.

'Not that you can stop me, exactly, but no, I wasn't planning on jumping ship. Well, only so far as I intend it to be my own ship.'

His eyes narrowed. 'Explain.'

'I don't intend to sit around twiddling my thumbs while you jet off wherever. I'm… I'm starting a women's empowerment charity.' She held her breath, waiting for signs of mockery. When surprisingly it didn't arrive, she pressed on. 'I'm in the process of setting up preliminary meetings.'

Surprise lit his eyes but again it was overshadowed by deep wariness. 'Kudos to you. But you won't exert yourself and harm the child.'

She breathed through the twin sensations of being touched that he cared but dismayed that the care was mainly for his child.

'First of all, we don't even know if there is a child,' she replied, even though her certainty grew firmer by the second.

Especially since yesterday had come and gone with no sign of her period.

'Even if there is, the *child* is barely even a bundle of cells right now. Women have been known to work right up until birthing a child, you know.'

A healthy fraction of that primal gleam he'd delivered

that day by the stream lit his eyes. 'I don't care about other women.'

They both froze at that, their gazes clashing for several seconds before yanking away to redirect elsewhere. She absolutely wasn't going to read anything into that. Hell, hadn't he spelled out that he could never care for her only a week or so ago?

This was all about the child she might be carrying.

Mareka struggled to contain the hurt and busied herself cutting up the fruit on her plate while Cayetano poured himself an espresso. Tossing it back, he immediately poured himself another. This one he nestled in the saucer, his fingers absently caressing the delicate cup. She envied him the ability to ingest so much caffeine, knowing she'd be a hyperactive wreck if she even tried more than one cup. Could she even drink coffee now?

'What are you thinking?' he asked abruptly.

She flicked him a wary glance, then blurted, 'Coffee. I was wondering if I could drink it if I'm...'

His green gaze dropped to her belly for a split second. 'You can, in small amounts. But decaf is best for pregnant women.'

'You've read up on the diet for a good pregnancy?'

He arched his eyebrow. 'You think I would not?'

She wasn't ready to admit how strongly that affected her heart and how it foolishly leapt with something close to joy. 'Like I said, we don't know one way or another yet.'

Another throb of silence echoed between them, then he reached beneath the newspaper. 'This was delivered for you half an hour ago.' He set down a rectangular package next to her plate. 'If my guess is right as to what it contains, then you're as eager to know as I am.'

At her raised brow, he produced a glossy paper bag

which had been out of sight near his feet. Peering into it, she saw several pregnancy tests. 'You bought five? I got two.'

His powerful shoulders shrugged. 'Between us we have enough to make sure without a shadow of doubt, no?'

Her fingers shook as she reached for her juice. 'We…?' Of course he planned to be part of this. 'I thought you would be too busy.'

His lips firmed. 'You continue to make assumptions. Be careful, *querida*: I will only indulge you so far. Now, finish your breakfast.'

He passed her a bowl of fruit. She wanted to refuse his order on principle, but the orange and peach segments looked too succulent to resist. Still, she tossed him a glare, which he responded to with a conceited arched brow before he picked up his tablet.

The moment she was done, he rose and pulled back her chair. Every step of the way back upstairs, her heart clamoured in her chest. On the last step, she stumbled. Strong, firm hands caught her, his sharp inhale echoing in the large space.

'Tranquilo.'

She glanced at him. He'd lost a shade of colour but otherwise he remained as suave and in control as she was flustered.

'Thanks.'

His response was a brisk nod, his gaze fixed on her bedroom door as he led her inside. She felt his tension as he dropped his hands and shoved them into his pockets. She'd thought he'd start pacing but he stopped in the middle of her bedroom, a formidable presence awaiting an outcome he hadn't anticipated.

She learned that outcome five minutes later, three of

the seven tests announcing that she was indeed pregnant. And when she opened the door he only needed one look at her face to know.

A shudder went through him, and he lost another layer of colour. But Cayetano Figueroa, the man she was indelibly tied to for the rest of her life, strode forward an instant later, the epitome of power and control. 'My doctor will be in touch with you today. He'll arrange for a blood test and the necessary pre-natal regime. And I presume you'll want to keep this confidential for now?'

'I...yes. But don't you want to discuss...anything else?'

His eyes narrowed with suspicion. 'Anything like what? You're carrying my child. In nine months, you'll deliver it and we will endeavour to be the best parents we can be. There's nothing more to discuss.'

Oh, yes, there was...so much more. But she knew she was in shock, despite having fully braced herself for just this outcome. So, when he closed the gap between her and caught her chin in his hand, Mareka could do nothing but stare at him.

'Mareka...'

'What?'

He exhaled long and slowly. 'I'm leaving now. The housekeeper and the rest of the staff will be on hand if you need anything.'

He seemed to be waiting for something as he continued to stare down at her. At her jerky nod, his lips firmed. Then, obviously accepting she wasn't about to speak, Caye dropped his hand and walked out.

Mareka stumbled over to the bed and sank down onto it. She was going to be a mother—most likely, a single mother. Because, even this early on, she knew there was no way she could continue with this clinical marriage with

Cayetano when the three years were up. Hell, he might want his freedom long before that.

She released a shaky breath and this time, when her hand stole over her belly, she allowed it to rest, allowed the feeling to settle and sink deep. Then she made solemn, silent promises to her unborn child—promises to protect, love, nurture and defend it, no matter what.

Awed and purpose-filled, Mareka was composed and waiting when the doctor arrived two hours later. She couldn't dwell on the fact that she missed Cayetano's presence with an acuteness that was terrifying and shocking. She would wean this rabid need. *She had to.*

Alone again, she spent another afternoon on her laptop, working with a few breaks until a shadow fell over her. She looked up to find Cayetano standing next to the lounger. 'You're back.'

His face shuttered. 'You don't need to sound so disappointed.'

'I'm…not. I'm just surprised…' She looked around. The sun was just starting to go down. 'I thought you'd be late, that's all.'

'I'm told you've been out here all day.' There was light censure in his tone.

She bristled, then hated how that made her feel *alive*. How his masculine scent washing over her made her want to take huge, gulping breaths. 'Your spy network is on point, I see.'

His sculpted features grew stonier. 'You wish to fight, *guapa*, despite the specifically heated way our skirmishes end?' he asked in a dangerously silken voice.

And, as she was floundering in blazing recollection, he hitched up his trousers and settled down on the lounger next to hers. Feeling her bikini-clad body's Pavlovian re-action, she pulled up her knees and wrapped her arms around them. 'What do you want?' she muttered.

The flash of ire mingled with something that looked like…hurt disappointment. 'To see how the appointment with the doctor went. And to invite you to lunch tomor-row.'

Paradoxically, the giddiness of her reaction to his in-vitation made her glad to be able to say, 'I can't. I'm busy tomorrow. One of the women who runs the international STEM foundation for young girls is in town. I'm meet-ing with her.'

'Already?'

'You doubt my efficiency?'

'If I did, *guapa*, you wouldn't have been working for me.'

She cursed the blush that heated her face, just as she cursed the sardonic amusement that twitched in his. 'Should I say thanks or is this another interrogation to see if I'm going to be overdoing things?'

Amusement vanished, a hard glint entering his eyes. 'Hate me if you must, but there will be a level of over-sight into your activities over the next nine months. But, in this case, I was merely pointing out that it's time for another public appearance.'

Another wave of heat came, this one of pure embar-rassment, washed away her foolish giddiness. Of course he was doing it only for appearances' sake. 'Oh. Well, I'm sorry to disappoint you, but I can't cancel. I'm lucky to have caught her.'

The tightness didn't lessen, but again a curious look filmed his eyes. Surprise? Admiration? Sure she was imagining it, she pulled her glance away, just as he murmured, 'Perhaps she's lucky to have caught *you*.'

Her gaze jerked back to him, that warmth she hoped she'd caged for good blooming wild and unfettered inside her.

For the longest beat, they stared at one another, their breaths growing increasingly loud in the silence. When his gaze dropped down her face, lingered on her mouth and fell lower to her chest, Mareka's heart pumped. And within that cocoon of swirling emotions she began to wonder if, perhaps even accept that, the fascination she held for this man might never be contained. That, despite all her efforts, the crush she'd hoped to snuff out had against her will blossomed into something *more*, something highly detrimental to her emotional wellbeing.

'Mareka?' Her name was filled with a thousand questions and a million warnings, as if he *knew*.

It'll be a mistake to develop feelings for me...

She jerked her head away again, tightening her own features so she didn't give herself away. 'Like I said, I can't make it tomorrow.'

She knew him well enough to sense his displeasure and, for some reason, it didn't irritate her. Instead, she was delighted. Was she really that desperate for any crumb of attention that she would rejoice even when she couldn't take advantage of it?

'How many meetings have you planned?'

'One more this week, then another two next week.'

His jaw clenched. Silence stretched her nerves to the breaking point, a punch of pride stopping her from offering another date. Then she blinked away confused tears when she sensed him rise, his stare drilling into her.

'We will have to make the best of the time we have

together, then,' he drawled. 'At the very least, breakfasts and dinners together. Without fail.' Edict delivered, he walked away, his heavy footsteps echoing her heartbeat.

That set the tone for the two next months.

They ate their first and last meals together, whether they were in Buenos Aires or, as Mareka chose after a brief discussion, at the Cordoba ranch when she didn't have face-to-face meetings. At each meal, Cayetano quizzed her about her health, the depth of his attention almost giving the illusion that he cared.

Almost. Because, on their unavoidable social engagements, he was courteous and cordial, drawing her into conversations long enough to satisfy the avid watchers that they were very much a united front. But the second the spotlight dimmed he retreated, his arm dropping, his face tautening.

The day the morning sickness arrived with cyclone force, she wasn't at all stunned when he made an appearance an hour after breakfast. She'd long suspected Cayetano's staff was reporting her every move to him.

'What are you doing here?' she croaked, drained with throwing up and chagrined that he had to see her like this when he looked so vitally healthy. *So damn magnificently male!*

He set a tray holding tea and dry crackers on her lap, sending a hard look at her laptop before pouring her a cup. 'You continue to doubt that I intend to be an equal partner in this?'

'I continue to feel like the glass case holding crown jewels—useful but not ultimately important.' The reply was drenched in bitterness she couldn't hold back.

He stiffened. 'What do you mean?'

Harsh laughter seared her throat. 'You know very well what I mean. You play the caring husband in public because you don't want your father or anyone to challenge your right to your company. You're here now because you think you need to safeguard this pregnancy.'

'I do not—'

'Yes, you do. "Are you well?" "Are you resting enough?" "Has the doctor prescribed something for the morning sickness?"' she snapped. 'Remind me when you last asked me anything to do with me instead of this baby?'

He stiffened harder, but she shook her head before he could supply a response that would no doubt confirm her position as a disposable cog in his life. 'Believe it or not, this baby is as important to me as it to you. Maybe even more.'

Tense silence came, then, 'What's that supposed to mean?'

'It means you didn't want children with me, or even want them at all. They were just an abstract possibility in your future. But, now you don't have a choice but to face fatherhood, you're treating me like a delicate flower you need to watch carefully in case I fail. I was quite capable of taking care of myself before you came along and I intend to take even better care of this baby. So you can carry on with your essential empire-building and leave me be.'

An even longer stretch of charged silence ensued, during which she squeezed her eyes shut and clutched her tea cup.

'The child you're carrying is now part of my so-called empire building,' he stated with frigid tones. 'A vital component, in fact. So, no, *tesoro*, I will not take a back seat. I will see you tonight at dinner if you wish to fight again.'

She stayed in her room for dinner that night, mostly because it turned out morning sickness wasn't just restricted to mornings, and also because part of her wanted to see his reaction to her defiance.

Because in the past it had turned up the heat in ways that set her heart racing in recollection...

Dressing for her appointment with the head of an international women's charity the next morning, Mareka refused to accommodate that whispered opinion. She had young women to help empower, lives she hoped to make better with a fraction of the support she'd had a decade ago.

And she most definitely wasn't going to think about the emails she'd sent her parents two weeks ago with her pregnancy news that were still unanswered. She'd felt a mixture of anxiety and joy when she'd sent them, hoping for a crumb of regard to bolster her. Had she been tech-savvy she would've recalled them. But maybe it was a good thing. Maybe it was time to finally accept that, as Cayetano had warned about feelings for him, there was no point harbouring deep emotions for her parents. She was in this alone. And she would endeavour to thrive, despite everything.

She selected a bold orange sheath dress, taking advantage of form fitting clothes while she still could. Blow-drying her hair, she left it loose and, on a wild whim, went with a bold red lipstick. Confidence boosted, she snatched up the clutch bag that matched her heels.

Forty minutes later, her third deal on starting a foundation for young women in business in London and Tahiti was agreed. Mareka had just finished signing on the dotted line when a hush came over the Michelin-starred restaurant in which she was dining. Glancing round, her nape started to tingle wildly with awareness, her heart-beat accelerating.

Even before he came into view, she knew the reason for her body's wild reaction. Sure enough, Cayetano strode into the restaurant, making a beeline for her with purpose brimming his face and body. When he reached her, he lowered his head and took her mouth in a brazen kiss that drew several gasps.

He nodded to the CEO, whose eyes were lingering much too appreciatively on Cayetano, before turning to Mareka's. 'Don't let me disturb you, *guapa*,' he said in a deep, seductive drawl that had her thighs clenching.

She smothered a snort. As if *anyone* in the world could ignore him. With another brush of his lips at her temple, she watched, eyes wide and most likely displaying many more feelings than she wished to, as he parked himself at the next table, murmuring to the waiter who'd hurried over to him, without breaking his focus on her.

Composure became a struggle as she finished her meeting. The moment it ended and the older woman left, Cayetano rose and sauntered over, every set of eyes in the restaurant following his powerful, breath-taking form.

'What are you doing here?' she whispered fiercely under her breath when he leaned over to brush a leisurely hand over her heated cheek.

'Surprising my wife in a lovely restaurant to celebrate her impressive new business deal. What else?'

'But we didn't…this isn't a scheduled engagement.'

'What can I say? I missed you. Enough for me to cancel my appointments to come see you.'

The words were delivered with enough acerbity for her to know he didn't mean them. And yet her heart leapt before she could stop herself. 'You mean you're here because

I missed dinner last night and breakfast this morning?' she murmured, conscious of their audience.

His eyes glittered. 'Wasn't that what you were hoping for? For me to dance to your tune?' he drawled.

'You've never danced to anyone's tune in your life.'

His shrug was far too sexy and distracting. And she'd missed it, including the arrogance and curious heaviness it came with. 'Life has a way of surprising us.'

Her breath strangled in her lungs, foolish hope unfurling deep within. 'What does that mean?'

He seemed to debate his answer, a perplexed expression crossing his face before he shrugged. 'Don't overthink it, *tesoro*. Ah, here's the waiter with the wine now.'

The alcohol-free sparkling wine he poured and passed to her, coupled with his words of congratulations, fizzed its way through her, making a mockery of the undeniable fact that all this was a performance for him—that their audience was lapping it up and the tabloids would undoubtedly write reams about Cayetano lavishing his new wife with champagne and attention.

For the next half hour, while he repeatedly trailed his hand over her arm, toyed with a lock of her hair and tortured her with his devastating smile and intoxicating scent, she smiled as several prominent people dropped by, eager to be seen with the great Cayetano Figueroa.

Eventually, her starched smile threatening to split her face, she grabbed her clutch bag. 'If we're quite done with National Paw Your Wife Day, can we leave, please?'

His sexy smile remained in place but the hard glint in his eyes reflected his true feelings. 'More like Show the World You Can't Keep Your Hands Off Your Sexy Wife Day. And I think that mission is thoroughly accomplished, don't you?'

Her face was on fire and she knew she was still the focus of every pair of eyes. 'Whatever you do, please do not run your hand over my belly when we get outside. I think that would be one cliché too far and I can do without the rabid tabloid speculation.'

For a long moment, she thought he would do it just to spite her. 'I recall a time when you screamed yourself hoarse for my touch.'

'Well, I think we both agree that was a brief moment of madness.'

A muscle ticked in his jaw and his eyes turned so dark and volatile, her heart caught. A moment later he regained his control. 'I'll grant your wish only because you beg so beautifully,' he said, dry mockery abrading her skin. 'And because I won't be around to shield you from the gutter rats.'

Her breath caught and her heart dropped in alarming dismay. 'You're leaving?'

He gave a brisk nod, his face still a mask of tempered fury. 'I'm due in China for a two-week set of deal closings.'

'Two weeks?' She hated the squeak in her voice.

Serious green eyes trailed her face before his lips twisted. 'Yes. So, I guess you'll have the freedom you've been craving. You won't need to be worried about your husband laying his unwanted hands on you.'

His caustic reply made her flinch, but Mareka was more interested in why she stupidly yearned to ask why he wasn't inviting her to come with him, despite the charged atmosphere between them. Despite being a wife who accompanied him on his business trips not being part of their deal.

'You have no response to that?' he demanded, the acid throb in his voice intensifying.

Yes, she wanted to yell. *Take me with you. Because, despite everything that has happened, I'll miss you terribly.*

Thankfully, she managed to trap the words inside and maintain her composure even as yearning swelled and threatened to suffocate her.

'Will you be back for the ultrasound?' she blurted as he led her outside, where their respective drivers stood next to their cars.

Cayetano froze, his eyes darting to her belly before returning to her face. A wild, visceral flash crossed his face. 'You want me there?' There was a thread she couldn't fathom in the question. And, because she didn't want to hang foolish, heart-bruising speculation on it, she pushed it away.

'Can I stop you?'

The last vestiges of cordiality vanished, leaving him a proud, stiff pillar of censure. 'No. In this too, you cannot.'

Some part of her knew she only had herself to blame for this streak of niggling she couldn't seem to stop. The other part of her welcomed it. Maybe this separation would be what she needed to apply the brakes on this emotional runaway train before it was too late.

If it wasn't already...

CHAPTER ELEVEN

HIS WIFE HATED the sight of him.

It was a truth that shouldn't have mattered one iota and yet it interrupted Cayetano's sleep and his waking moments. It kept him off-kilter in a way that both infuriated and shockingly bewildered him.

He was especially resentful that it threatened every deal he'd sought to finalise for the next two months, long after he'd returned from China. His board members and staff had been terrorised and he knew they were glad to see the back of him when he joined Mareka in Cordoba. His inability to focus in itself made him a nightmare to be around.

It didn't help that every conversation with Mareka was like drawing blood from stone. It would've helped if he could have stayed away from her, but the little witch had cast a spell on him. So here he was in Cordoba, waiting for her to return from another meeting in Buenos Aires while he battled with this unfathomable ache in his chest.

He poured himself a drink, then activated the app which showed him the security cameras at his Buenos Aires home. Scrolling through that morning's feed, he paused repeatedly on images of Mareka. She'd developed a deeper tan in the last few weeks. Her hair had grown longer too, the gold tints bleached lighter, making her glow even more breath-taking.

He paused on a video of her by the pool, her voluptuous body sporting the sexiest bikini he'd ever seen. It was almost scandalous, the way the white fabric clung to her skin. And were her breasts larger?

Cayetano swallowed, his hand drifting down to his swelling shaft before he hissed in annoyed frustration and killed the motion. *Dios mio*, he wasn't a hormonal teenager, slobbering over a scantily dressed woman, even if that woman was his gorgeous, disagreeable wife!

A wife who'd proved to be a formidable champion of young women in the very short time since she'd got her charity up and running. The Mareka Figueroa Women's Empowerment Charity—and, yes, he'd experienced a punch of pride that she'd used his name—had already made impressive strides in education, sports and small business funding in a handful of deprived countries.

Far from being the gold-digger his father had labelled her, she'd directed every cent of the million dollars he'd given her into her charity. And she was fast turning into a media darling. He'd watched his wife handle tough journalists with aplomb but, even as he'd been awed by her, he'd felt the hollow ache within him intensify. She was giving him exactly what he'd asked for—an emotionless union meant to fool the world—yet Cayetano hated it.

Closing the app with a tight, self-deprecating curse, he started the call he'd been placing daily—not to his wife this time, but to his housekeeper. Relief swelled through him once the report had been delivered.

Yes, the *señora* was well.

Yes, she'd spent a few hours by the pool, then had attended her meeting.

Yes, she'd thrown up only once and her appetite was returning.

No, she hadn't asked about the *señor*.

He clenched his jaw at that last one, blaming himself for giving in to the urge to ask. Hadn't he learned his lesson from the way his own parents treated him? But... was he being disingenuous? Hadn't Mareka given him a glimpse of what being cared about looked like and hadn't he shut it down?

With a rough growl, he tossed the phone aside, shrugging out of his suit. About to undo his shirt, he leapt for the phone again when it rang. But it wasn't who he'd hoped it would be. Another, louder growl left his throat when he saw Octavia's name on the screen. He wasn't ready to deal with her drama and he took petty pleasure in declining the call. Her nose had been wrenched severely out of joint when he'd suggested she make use of the many weeks of accrued vacation time, and maybe even take an extended break.

Just now, the only person he wanted to deal with was his wife. Against all his lofty assertions about being above emotion, he'd developed an obsession for the wife he'd hired to secure his birthright, and for the baby she carried.

As he stood beneath the umpteenth cold shower he'd taken in the last several weeks, he couldn't help but accept that it was a state of affairs that he'd never seen coming and that he was at a complete loss as to how to combat it effectively.

'Thank you, everyone. I promise I'll visit soon.'

Mareka ended the video-conference to a chorus of

cheers, with a tremulous smile and tears in her eyes. The crown jewel in her ambitions—the education foundation in Papeete, Tahiti—had officially been opened. The moment she logged off, her hand dropped to her stomach, the need to connect with her baby a powerful draw. But, as had been happening shockingly frequently, a deep ache immediately replaced her joy. While she was ecstatic about fulfilling her dreams, the more she achieved, the more acutely she felt the loss in her own life.

Despite travelling along the road to empowering others' lives, the love she lacked in hers glared as bright as the neon lights she'd ignored before.

Specifically, the love of her husband.

The husband who'd warned her against developing feelings for him. The husband she now knew she loved with every fibre of her being. Perhaps if Cayetano had maintained the distance she'd riled against, she could've salvaged something from the pieces of her heart that had recklessly delivered themselves into his undesiring hands.

Instead, with his presence at most mealtimes, every gruff enquiry about her health and about their baby, with every compliment he made about her charity work that announced that he was keeping tabs on that, sparks of hope and joy fired within her, defying every attempt to suppress it.

Lately, with her baby growing stronger and bigger each day, Mareka had started to wonder if things needed to stay the way they'd agreed. Whether she could make another dream come true...

Maybe it was the reserves of strength and self-worth she'd discovered within herself recently. Whatever it was, the ultrasound was scheduled for tomorrow. Cayetano had stayed true to being present for every step of this pregnancy.

Maybe this was her chance…

Her thoughts were disrupted when Ariana—the housekeeper whom she'd discovered was married to the butler—appeared with a wide smile, a tray of Mareka's favourite punch and a selection of *tucumanas* and *pastafrolas*. The older woman had cheekily admitted she was under orders from Cayetano to keep a close eye on her. It meant Mareka was cheerfully chivvied into eating and resting at strictly regular intervals.

Ariana's clear delight at her task had warmed Mareka, as had the priceless advice about pregnancy the housekeeper, with her ten grandchildren, had passed on.

'I'm going to become as big as a house if I keep this up,' Mareka complained, reaching for her second *tucumana*. The empanadas were heavenly, and deceptively bite-sized, and she devoured four before she put on the brakes.

'The *señor* will be pleased, *si*?' Ariana said, her gaze sharpening on Mareka's face.

'Yes… *Si*…' she echoed distractedly, her heart banging against her ribs, her mind racing at the idea which grew as Ariana bustled about for another minute before leaving her alone. The feeling that this was a pivotal moment in her relationship with Cayetno wouldn't leave her. And, despite the potentially painful outcome, she took extra care in dressing up before meeting Cayetano in the living room, where he awaited the doctor's arrival.

Her pulse was racing when she stepped into the room ten minutes later dressed in an emerald-green jersey dress with capped sleeves that loosely moulded her body. Yes, it turned out her favourite colour in her new wardrobe was still green.

He looked up when she entered, then rose and crossed the room to her. 'Are you well?'

Her heart dipped but she breathed through the trepidation because Mareka wanted to believe it meant something. That, if nothing else, she'd over-exaggerated the depths of his detachment.

'Yes,' she answered in a husky, breathless tone she decided she wasn't going to be embarrassed about. Where had guarding her heart got her? It had ignored all her fight and deepened her crush into love.

Maybe it was time to be brave. Time to...to... She bit her lip, the last defences unwilling to be dislodged just yet. 'You?'

Faint, bleak spectres danced across his face before disappearing. Then one corner of his mouth quirked up, a shrug following it. 'A few skin-of-the-teeth challenges, but nothing that couldn't be handled in the end.'

She nodded, cleared her throat and dragged her gaze from his far too distracting face and body—a body she'd missed with every fibre of her being. 'That's...umm... great.'

Awkward silence floundered between them, then he gave a low, mocking laugh, his face slowly hardening until it was an emotionless mask. 'Is this really that difficult for you—looking your husband in the face and having a simple conversation?'

Her gaze darted up. 'W-what? That's not what I'm doing at all. I'm... I was...' Her words froze when Ariana knocked and entered. The older woman's gaze swung between them, a flash of concern crossing her face before she spoke to Cayetano in rapid-fire Spanish.

He murmured back, his gaze never leaving Mareka.

'The doctor is here,' he said after Ariana exited. 'At least in this we can be united, *si*?'

Feeling the ground crack and tilt beneath her, but equally at a loss as to how to stop it, she nodded. Cayetano started to step forward then, frowning, he turned, gesturing her towards the door. She sailed ahead of him, viciously aware of his gaze on her, aware of the subtle changes in her body. Her breasts had grown heavier, her hips fuller. Even her skin felt that little bit more vibrant. Did he notice?

She shook her head, impatient with herself for her desperate thoughts. But that bleakness in his eyes flashed through her mind again and, as she was readied for the first glimpse of the life she carried, Marcka couldn't stop herself from glancing at Caye, from searching for further insights into how he truly felt. The look he returned was inscrutable, devastatingly characteristic of the ruthless, formidable magnate who conquered worlds before 9:00 a.m. each morning.

There was no give at all...until the sound of their baby's heartbeat echoed through the quiet room. She felt a shudder ripple through his body braced close to hers on the portable examination bed. Then his jaw sagged, his chest rising and falling rapidly as his avid gaze flew to the 3D screen.

An awed gasp left Mareka as she watched the tiny expressions chase across her baby's face, tiny fingers starfishing as it moved.

'*Dios mio,*' Cayetano rasped, a thick exhale moving through him. 'She...he...is...'

Relieved and moved by his emotion, that this pillar of self-control was lost for words, Mareka placed her hand on top of his. He startled, then his awed gaze found hers. 'I know.'

He swallowed, his gaze sweeping her face as the doctor smiled indulgently, clicked on a few buttons and nodded. 'Everything seems to be in order. You can carry on as normal, Señora Figueroa.'

Another wave of relief swept through her and, when Caye's fingers meshed with hers, she couldn't help but tighten her grip and allow a sliver of hope to filter through her defences.

Maybe something positive could come out of this. They remained caught up in the tight cocoon of emotion as the doctor finished up, handed them images of their baby and quietly left. One of Cayetano's hands remained tightly on hers while the other brushed back the hair from her temple, then drifted down her cheek to caress her jaw. After staring into her eyes for an age, his hand drifted down to hover over her belly.

Another swallow moved his Adam's apple. 'I want… I need to touch you.' His voice was thick, stuffed full of emotions he'd claimed he didn't feel.

Her heart leapt, then she nodded before she could think better of it, before she could safeguard her heart. And, when his hand slid almost reverently over where their child nestled, she couldn't stop the soft gasp that shivered up from her throat at the reverence in the eyes that flew to meet hers. With mingled fear and hope rushing through her bloodstream, Mareka, blurted, 'Caye, I think we need to talk.'

He stiffened immediately, his jaw clenched as he abruptly removed his hand. She wanted to wail, to beg him to put it back. But she really was done begging for scraps, for love. She deserved more—unconditionally.

'Is this where you start to lay down ultimatums?' he ground out.

Her heart squeezed. She fought through it, rising from the bed so she didn't feel at such a disadvantage. 'Is that what you really think of me?' she challenged, her chin rising despite the despair swelling in her chest.

He withdrew further, aggressively shoving his hands into his pockets as if he despised himself for the need he'd just displayed. 'I've shown you how much I want my heir. You would be a fool not to recognise how much power that grants you.'

Pain slashed at the remnants of hope. 'That's what you would do in my shoes, is it?'

His face darkened at her taunt, then he shrugged. 'I can't help but remember that we got here in the first place because we were both getting something from each other.' He paused for a second, his gaze raking her face. 'Isn't that what you want to talk about? Something else you need from me?'

Yes, for you to love me!

But he'd effectively and cleverly cornered her. How could she ask for what she wanted now?

Are you going to give up that easily?

She wanted to hate that inner voice, but she couldn't deny that it had guided her heart's compass and ultimately been her companion for as long as she could remember. Perhaps now wasn't the time to reject it.

Sucking in another sustaining breath, she smoothed damp palms over her dress, unable to help her gaze from flicking to the bed. 'That moment just now, it wasn't some gateway for me to get leverage over you.'

Scepticism glinted in his eyes. 'Wasn't it?'

'Look, I know you hated showing your emotion like that…maybe because of your parents?'

When he stiffened further, she ploughed ahead. 'If you must know, I… I hate feeling like a spare part. Unless and until we can both deal with that, things will always feel… unbalanced. But I…'

He cursed something indecipherable under his breath, stopping her words. 'You're not a spare part.'

Years of residual bitterness swelled through her even as warmth filtered through at his response. But she'd been here far too often to let it linger. 'Tell that to my parents who didn't want me in academia because, if I failed, I'd be an embarrassment—and, if I succeeded, would've been competition. But anything else outside their field was considered a failure anyway.'

Fury flashed across his face. 'They told you that?'

'Not in so many words. But I discovered my mother's diary from her honeymoon when she realised she was pregnant with me. And…it was…it wasn't fairy-tale reading for a nine-year-old, I'll tell you that much. I was an obligation, a useless extension of themselves they had to endure then, and that never changed. Tell me how any child is supposed to navigate that,' she said in a strained voice, then shook her head. 'I've never told that to anyone.'

If she'd been expecting sympathy, she was to be disappointed. His face remained clenched. 'And you feel you're not able to stop history repeating itself?' he demanded tightly.

Determination charged through her, and she shook her head definitively. 'Not if I can help it. I know what it feels not to be wanted. I intend to make sure my child never feels that way. I want this baby more than anything. I can only hope that my own experiences help remind me of what not to do.'

He looked startled for a moment, then his expression grew even darker. 'Do I hear judgement in there somewhere, *guapa*?'

'You accused me of putting words in your mouth once. I'm only speaking for myself. I know I'm not perfect, that my childhood has probably damaged me—'

Another expletive interrupted her. 'Stop saying that about yourself. In fact, I think it's done the opposite.'

'It's hard not to when I told them I was having a baby weeks ago and they haven't bothered to respond. Or that my last phone call went to voicemail.'

He shrugged. 'That's their problem. You're the polar opposite of those...coldly detached people who attended our wedding.'

Then why don't you want me?

Luckily, the words remained trapped deep inside her. Realising after a minute that he was waiting for her to continue, Mareka cleared her throat. 'What I'm saying is, there's no need for this...strain between us. I...um... reread the agreement. It said that, if we both agree that we can't make it work, then we can go our separate ways or we can re...'

His cynical laugh stopped her. 'Despite your protests, you're proving me right after all.'

'Would you let me finish, please?'

He lunged forward, his movements almost frantic, his body blotting out the light as he stopped an arm's length away. 'Why, when I know what you're going to say? You're either going to threaten to leave me, or demand custody, or you're going to renegotiate better financial terms. The answer to all of it is no. You would've found out by now that charity doesn't come cheap. I doubt the last thing you'll want is to let down all the people you've pledged to help. That alone should keep you where you are—as my wife—until our agreement is honoured.'

Her heart squeezed tighter. 'Cayetano, don't—'

His hand flew out of his pocket to silence her with a halting gesture. 'It doesn't have to be all bad right now. As of this morning, I've instructed my lawyers to match what you've spent on your foundation so far. But keep threatening to renege on our deal in any way, and I'll stop it. Is that clear?'

'It really is all about gaining the upper hand with you, isn't it?'

His gaze dropped to her belly and heavy emotion moved through his eyes. 'No, *pequeña*. It's also now about claiming what's mine. Like you, my parents have taught me a lesson—that I can't rely on anyone but myself. So this is ensuring that nothing is ever given or taken away from me that I can't control.'

'You do realise that I can walk away at any time, don't you? Even if it's just to prove to you that I don't want your precious money—that it's clear that you can't give me what I want.'

Green eyes turned black. 'You shouldn't test me like this, *guapa*,' he warned silkily. Then, reaching into his pocket, he drew out his phone. The instruction to his driver, despite being spoken in Spanish, was clear enough.

'You're leaving?'

'It's clear my presence here isn't good for either of us— or the baby. I think it's best to carry on with that empire-building you accused me of. *Hasta luego, tesoro.*'

The coolly drawled goodbye finally broke her. 'You can't just walk out!'

A mocking glance over his shoulder seared her as he sauntered towards the door. 'Can't I? How are you going to stop me?'

'God, you…you bastard!'

He stiffened for a moment, but he didn't turn round, nor did he stop.

Five minutes later, she stood at the window, shock, pain and terror spiking through her as she watched Cayetano drive off.

The handful of times she and Cayetano met over the next six weeks were painful in a way Mareka had hoped never to experience again. It was also clear she'd only experienced a less devastating version of rejection from her parents.

But, conversely, in those six weeks she learned a great deal about herself. She knew that what she'd said to him that last day was right—she wanted her baby fiercely. She was willing to and *could* do anything in her power to create a loving and happy home, one her parents had never bothered to give her. And, when she tried one last time to contact her parents and only received a lukewarm, 'We wish you the best with it,' she decided to save herself further heartache and shelve what was clearly an unsalvageable relationship. Whatever happened in the future with them, for now she needed to make herself and her baby her priority.

But, more and more, the voice at the back of her mind urged her that there was one relationship she owed it to herself and her baby to try to salvage one more time.

'It's lunch time!'

Mareka looked up as Luna, her new assistant, bustled into her office and set down a tray front of her. The chicken salad looked delicious, but the nerves churning through her stopped her reaching for the food.

'Something wrong?' Luna asked, the layer of anxiety that seemed to cloak the younger girl, thickening.

When Mareka had accepted she couldn't efficiently take on her foundation's responsibilities all by herself, she'd been adamant about surrounding herself with women who needed the help her charity would provide. Luna's background of escaping domestic abuse and her determination to find self-worth beyond that had made it a no-brainer for Mareka to hire her. But Luna occasionally regressed, letting anxiety overwhelm her—something with which Mareka empathised.

'Not with the food, no,' she responded, then smiled at Luna's palpable relief. 'But I need your help with something.'

'*Si*…anything,' Luna responded enthusiastically.

Mareka bit the inside of her lip, wondering whether she had it in her to take the course she was contemplating.

Yes. This was too important to prevaricate about.

Sucking in a deep breath, she let it out slowly. Then she said, 'My husband is on a business trip. I'd like you to book me a plane ticket to join him.'

Luna's eyes widened, as most people's did when Cayetano's name was mentioned. With a little excited squeak that would've amused Mareka if she hadn't been shrivelling inside with nerves, her assistant all but flew out of the room to do her bidding.

CHAPTER TWELVE

She landed in New York City sixteen hours later, and the car service Luna had organised for her whisked her away from JFK to Manhattan just before sundown. She'd taken pains to ensure her visit remained a secret. Or at the very least as last-minute as possible.

Was it because she'd been terrified Cayetano would stop her? Or, even worse, detail exactly *why* he didn't want her anywhere near him?

Yes to both!

Even now, two hours after arriving at the hotel she'd requested because it was one block from Cayetano's luxury penthouse, she couldn't stem the apprehensive tremors rippling through her body as she dressed.

The soft cream jersey midi-dress gently draped her body and showed off her rounded belly. A rich cashmere coat of the same length and colour completed the classy look, the combo bolstering her confidence.

She had a crucial hour's window in Cayetano's breakneck appointment schedule and, as much as she wanted to give up, she knew she couldn't return to Buenos Aires without taking this chance.

Securing diamond studs in her ears after several shaky tries, she added a platinum-and-diamond bracelet she'd only spotted recently in her jewellery collection but which had quickly become her favourite. The chain was delicate, the gem modest enough for Mareka to wear on a daily basis without feeling grossly ostentatious.

Slipping her feet into simple pumps, she snatched up her matching coffee-coloured clutch bag. As she descended in the lift, every sinew in her body pleaded with her to change her mind, to opt out of impending heartache. But then she caught sight of her reflection in the polished silver interior of the lift and saw the proof of her determination.

This was why: she owed it to her baby to try.

Did she want to do this on her own if she didn't have to? *What about your heart? The protection of not living in perpetual heartache?*

The walk ended quicker than she wished, the courteous doorman at the iconic New York skyscraper holding the glass door open for her, giving her no other choice but to step through.

The shiny chrome, polished glass and Modernist decor was a world removed from the deep comfort and elegance of Cayetano's homes in Argentina but it was no less jaw-dropping. Before she chickened out and changed her mind, she hurried to the lift and pressed the button for the penthouse. Before she could catch her breath, the lift ascended with smooth efficiency and spat her out half a minute later into a private foyer.

To be greeted with the towering, thin-lipped, heartrendingly beautiful form of her husband, arms folded.

'This is unexpected.' The statement was weighted with censure…and something puzzling. It was grim and probing, yet almost fatalistic. But she couldn't concentrate enough to decipher it because…*dear God*…despite his near-constant presence, she was starved of him. His hair was a little dishevelled, his five o'clock shadow making him positively sinfully attractive. Every cell in her body strained for this man she loved with terrifying ferocity.

'Mareka. Are you going to tell me why you've flown thousands of miles when I was due to fly back tomorrow?' Again, the mockery didn't quite pack much punch, as if his focus was pulled elsewhere.

His gaze did a lengthy survey of her body, pausing longest on her belly, then on the bracelet, the occasional enigmatic expression darting over his face. She yearned to ask him what he was thinking but, frankly, she was terrified.

Which left her with one option—to state her case so the chips could fall fast enough before she completely lost her nerve. 'We have a conversation to finish. And this time you're going to hear me out.' The words emerged more forcefully than she'd intended.

His eyes narrowed. 'I see you're emotional about something.'

'Yes, I'm emotional. I'm not a robot like you, Caye!'

For a blind moment, his eyes lit up with ice-cold fury. Then, fascinatingly, it disappeared layer by layer until there was nothing left. Nothing but the lines around his mouth deepening as his firm lips thinned. 'You're proving my point. You see why I can't permit myself to remain a slave to this…madness?'

'Why not?' she challenged. Maybe this was the perfect place to start—this madness that gripped them both.

He barked out a laugh, then shook his head. 'You want me to embrace something that has the potential to destroy me?'

'Not necessarily. Not if you look at it through another lens. If emotion brings you happiness, isn't that a good thing? You chase the high of impossible business deals every day. That's a different kind of love.'

'But business deals don't turn on me,' he insisted in a tone made of chilled steel. 'They don't manipulate, hold back or disappoint.'

She gasped. 'What's that supposed to mean? When have I done that to you? Or are you talking about someone else—your parents?'

His lips twisted then, turning on his heel, he went through double doors that led into a breath-taking living room. The views alone were to die for, but she was busy experiencing a different death.

'My parents no longer have that kind of power over me. But, with everyone else, it's always only a matter of time,' he said bitterly.

'And you can see into the future, can you?'

'No. But common sense follows that, based on a shocking number of failed relationships, that's where we're headed. Especially if the thing holding it together is purely physical.'

'Physical…' she echoed dismally. 'That's all you think we have?'

He shrugged. 'Perhaps a mutual responsibility for our child.' His dismissive hand slashed through his own response. 'Why are you here, Mareka?'

'I came to see if there was anything between us worth salvaging. But I've barely walked through the door and I have my answer.'

That bleakness shadowed his face again, then he exhaled. 'You should've called. I would've saved you a trip.'

And, just like that, the rug was pulled from under her every hope. 'God. You really are something, aren't you?'

His nostrils flared and she fully expected him to cut

her down. But, after a moment, he just shrugged again as if she wasn't even worth the effort. The last of her hope drained away.

'You said I wasn't a spare part but you can't wait to throw me away, can you? You know what you are? You're a coward.'

His whole body jerked, then he froze into an impregnable pillar. 'Watch it, *tesoro*.'

'Why, what have I got to lose? And don't you dare call me a treasure when you're treating me like dirt.'

'It's better this way.'

Her harsh laugh seared her throat and she feared the pain and bitterness coursing through her. But then she remembered that she'd been through this before. Certainly not as soul-destroying as this, but maybe, with the help of the love she intended to shower her baby with, she might not be completely annihilated. 'It's really not. And I feel sorry for you, because you'll only realise that when it's too late.'

He seemed poleaxed for a moment but of course, being Cayetano Figueroa, he eviscerated that weakness immediately. Watching her with a mocking smile, he folded his arms. 'Are you done?'

She glared at him. 'Why? Are you going to toss something conceited at me, like I need to calm down so I don't harm the baby?'

A charged look entered his eyes as his gaze dropped down to her body. 'I wouldn't dream of it. I have first-hand experience of how vibrant your passion can be. I only hope our son or daughter inherits it.'

She stared at him, nonplussed for a moment, before her heart reminded her of the risk she'd taken and how spectacularly she'd lost. She couldn't stay here. Fingers tightening around her clutch bag, she whirled and headed for the door.

'Where are you going?'

'Are you serious? What does it look like? I'm leaving.'

He arrived in front of her, not exactly barring her way, but not making it easy for her to go around him when his very presence was making her feel light-headed. Then she made the colossal mistake of swaying, her hand flying out to grab hold of something—anything. Unfortunately, the only solid thing was her husband.

With a thick curse, Cayetano caught and swept her into his arms, striding with purpose in the opposite direction of where she wanted to go.

'What are doing? Put me down!'

'Tranquilo, guapa.'

'No! I will not be *tranquilo.'*

He didn't listen to her, of course.

He entered a bedroom decked out in pale gold and silver furnishings, probably meant to soothe and comfort hard-working billionaires who didn't love their pregnant wives. He laid her down with precise gentleness, his breathing hardly affected, then stepped back swiftly, definitively.

'I have a meeting with my lawyers. It won't take long. I'll be back in two hours.' Those eyes seemed to search hers when he added, 'Then we can go home and address a few things.'

She swallowed the lump that charged into her throat, squashing the foolish, deadly hope that threatened to rise. Home was simply a place he laid his head. A place where he guarded his unborn child.

Home would never mean her.

For a long moment, his lashes veiled his expression

and, when he raised them, she thought she spotted flashes of bleakness steeped with desperate determination. But hadn't she been reading things from the very beginning that had only proved to be a mistake?

'You'll agree this limbo has gone on long enough, *si*?' he pressed.

Sorrow and pain rushed into the hollow spaces left by eviscerated hope. It was so debilitating, so all-encompassing, Mareka couldn't move. It was time to end this. Time to accept that they would never be. So she allowed him to believe her silence was acquiescence. Allowed him to fetch his phone and instruct the private kitchen to deliver far too much food. Allowed him to examine her critically as if he wanted to say much, much more. Then, when he decided she wasn't worth it, she allowed him to turn his back on her and walk away.

She tried so hard to catch the sobs that rumbled up from her soul the moment she was alone. When she failed, she succumbed to it, hoping to find rock bottom soon so she could reverse direction in time to save herself.

But rock bottom didn't come. Not in the next ten minutes or the half-hour that followed it. But the tears did run dry once she accepted it was over.

And *that* finally propelled her out of bed: shoes; bag; coat… A quick swipe of the vestiges of tears without the aid of a mirror because she couldn't face herself—not yet, not so soon. With a gulped in breath, and praying she wouldn't encounter anyone to witness the soulless, heartbroken shell of a person she'd become, Mareka stumbled out the back entrance of Cayetano's apartment building.

Back at her hotel, her case took minutes to pack, since she'd barely unpacked. Ten minutes later, she had checked out and was heading for the airport.

As with everything that had happened since she'd walked into the diamond emporium all those months ago, Mareka was stunned by how quickly events had unfolded. She'd left that place with a ring meant for another woman on her finger. She'd stepped into a role with all the naivety of a woman who believed she knew true suffering.

How wrong she'd been.

She stared down at the ring as her cab whisked her through the night back towards JFK. Maybe it was cursed. She half-snorted, half-sobbed, attracting the wary gaze of the driver. Partially hiding her face behind a tissue, she mopped up silent tears until the driver pulled up at the airport, relieved to be free of his emotionally addled passenger.

Inside, the ticket attendant's eyes widened when Mareka presented her passport. 'Oh, Mrs Figueroa, your return ticket to Buenos Aires isn't for another three days. If you want, I can—'

'No.' The decision was visceral. 'I'm not returning to Argentina. Can I change the destination?'

'Of course. Please give me a few minutes.'

She knew she was being accommodated because of who she was but Mareka didn't balk at it. Very soon, she would be back to being anonymous Mareka Dixon.

The sharp pain that lanced her heart made her gasp. And made the attendant's fingers dance that little bit faster over her keyboard.

Mareka booked herself a business class seat to London, because she couldn't risk the breakdown she sensed bubbling beneath her skin being aired on social media by an avid public equipped with smart phones if she sat in economy. On top of that, the last thing she needed was for rife speculation about why Cayetano's wife was travelling in economy and not on his private jet.

She grimaced at the eye-watering price and, with a silent promise to make up for it, she took her seat, thankful when, after a few attempts to discreetly engage her failed, the attendants left her alone.

Halfway across the Atlantic, lifting her hand to swipe away yet another tear, her wedding and engagement rings caught her eye and her heart snagged. Cayetano had gifted her the ring. But Mareka hadn't expected their agreement to end this soon.

They were so beautiful, she couldn't bear it. She *didn't* want to. Fishing in her bag, she felt her pulse race as she prayed she'd kept the embossed black card. When her fingers snagged on it, her breath shuddered in relief, then she bit her lip. The woman she'd met had been almost as formidable as Cayetano. Would she even be allowed inside the hallowed rooms of the diamond jeweller?

She could only try.

The anonymous donations amounting to five million dollars that had arrived in her charity's account over the last several weeks notwithstanding, she'd become shockingly aware of how much funding was needed to make a true difference. And, as much as she loved these rings, it was a much too painful and constant reminder of how she'd had the love of her life in her arms for one brief night before her heart had shattered into a million pieces.

She dialled the number, ignoring the text alerts and missed phone calls as another taxi drove her from Heathrow airport. Mareka considered going home to her old flat but she feared she'd only crawl beneath the covers and mope until her baby was ready to be born. So, clutching her phone and her suitcase, she sat on a park bench across from the jeweller's outwardly nondescript entrance in Knightsbridge and waited.

The ping arrived two hours later. Ms Smythe would see her at noon.

'Mrs Figueroa, this is…unusual,' the talented, mysterious jeweller said when Mareka stepped out of the lift at the designated time. There was no inflexion in her voice or expression in her eyes as to whether she was pleased or displeased about Mareka's request.

She was just as formidable a woman today as she'd been a few short, life-changing months ago. And it was those very life changes that powered up Mareka's chin when before she would've cowered. That made her smile and nod…

You're not a spare part.

She hated the clarity of Cayetano's voice in her head, the vivid recollection of those words to her. He'd helped her realise and own her self-worth. Then he'd shattered her.

Deep breath in, she slid the rings off her finger. 'Yes, and I'm sorry to just drop in like this.'

Ms Smythe's inscrutable eyes stayed on her. 'I said "unusual". If I didn't wish you to be admitted, you wouldn't be here.'

'Well, thank you.' Mareka cleared her throat and held out her hand. 'I'd like to return these. I'll take a reasonable below-market price for the inconvenience.'

'This isn't a back-street pawn shop, Mrs Figueroa.' Her tone was chilled but painfully cultured. 'You won't find some burly individual with false gold teeth trying to strong-arm you out of what your property is truly worth within these walls.'

Her gaze dropped to the rings and then to Mareka's

swollen belly. Something soft but heavy shifted in her eyes and the barest quiver fluttered her nostrils before she glanced back at the rings. 'Are you sure? Once I take possession of them, you won't get them back.'

Mareka pulled her longing gaze from the rings. They'd meant nothing but a means to an end for Cayetano. She couldn't let them mean anything to her.

'Yes, I'm sure.'

Ms Smythe nodded. 'Give me a moment to value them.' As she started to step away, her eyes dropped to Mareka's bracelet. 'That looks good on you.'

Surprise pulsed through her. 'This is one of yours?'

Perhaps she imagined the flash of pride in the other woman's eyes, and the ghost of a smile that fluttered over her lips, but the brisk nod was real. 'One of the pieces in my most recent commissioned collection. I wondered about...' She paused, seeming to catch herself.

Mareka jerked forward. 'What did you wonder about?'

Ms Smythe shook her head. 'That was uncalled-for speculation on my part. You must forgive...'

'Please.' She despised the needy quiver in her voice but she couldn't help it. 'I need to know.'

The way the woman's gaze brutally sized her up made Mareka pity anyone who was foolish enough to get in her way. And Mareka was just about ready to beg when the jeweller glanced down at the bracelet. 'I wondered about the inscription.'

Mareka frowned. 'What inscription?'

'*Esperanza eterna*: "hope eternal".'

The answer didn't come from Ms Smythe but from the deep, grave tones of the man she'd left in New York. In fact, by the time Mareka whirled to face Cayetano, the talented jeweller was already melting away, her movements as ephemeral as the muslin curtains that fluttered behind her when she disappeared.

Leaving Mareka alone with Cayetano, caught in the power of his seismic aura.

'What are you doing here?' One day in the future, she would stop sounding so breathless when she addressed him.

Green eyes rushed over her before latching onto her face. 'You left before I returned,' he said,

'And you followed me here? To do what—stop me because you're not quite done hurting me?'

His eyes darkened, a dramatic change that shocked her anew. 'Because your accusation was correct,' he delivered, his accent thickening. 'It was cowardly of me to leave things as they've been left.'

Mareka gasped, stung by guilt despite her shattered heart. 'No. What I said in New York wasn't…'

He exhaled and he seemed to cave in a little on himself, which was another shocking thing to witness. Enough to leave her speechless, even as he corrected that tiny error, his shoulders rearing back as he strode forward, a conqueror intent on stamping his will where he pleased. 'You were right—about all of it. I have been avoiding. And, if you hadn't come to see me, I would've kept on running.'

'Then shouldn't you be heading in the opposite direction?' she demanded, discovering she had reserves of bitterness within the sea of her heartache.

'No. Because while you were out of sight, but very much in mind, I hoped that you would remain with me, even held by the tenuous link of our agreement. But now…' He stopped his dark, bleak gaze dropping to the rings she'd dropped onto the square silk cushion. The

rings the mysterious jeweller had curiously left behind…
'Now I know. You're leaving me, aren't you?'

A sob shuddered its way up her soul. Thankfully, it stopped short before it totally humiliated her. 'I have to. I have no choice.'

He seemed to cave in once more, deeper this time, a haggard look shrouding his face. 'I blamed my grandfather for putting me in this position. I raged at his unreasonableness. But, underneath it all, the true reason I resisted was because of this very thing. This desperate hell of failing the one thing I suspected I would come to crave with every fibre of my being.'

The tremors weren't quite done with her, it seemed. 'W-what are you talking about?'

He took long, precise steps, as if caught on a string— one connected to her. 'You captivated me. You challenged me. You turned me on harder than any other woman. You terrified me with your passion. You took my seed into your body and you embraced the daunting possibility of parenthood while I ran scared. You overcame my every attempt for you not to become my first thought when I wake and the last before I sleep.'

'Cayetano…'

The shudder that seized her ricocheted through him, because apparently they were connected… 'You have no idea how I've longed to hear my name fall from your lips one more time, like that.'

'I still don't know what this means.'

'It means you've been asking me to prove myself one way or the other. Coming back to the penthouse and finding you gone… I can't keep running. It's killing me. So here I am, surrendering.'

The joy that had been creeping up on her stalled, then

rushed away. 'I don't want your surrender if it means you'll resent me for it down the line.'

He laughed, and when he spoke his voice was hoarse with untamed emotion. 'Give me the barest glimpse that you want me around and I'll never leave your side.'

She gasped. 'Cayetano. I don't... I...'

He surged another step closer. 'Tell me why you came to New York, *tesoro*.'

Because I want you to love me. The words screamed inside her, even now too terrified to emerge, in case this was all a fever dream.

'Please, Mareka. Tell me—was it to tell me you were leaving?'

This she could answer. 'No. It wasn't to leave you.'

But he wasn't satisfied because he was who he was: larger than life and unflinching about demonstrating it. 'But you're here now.' His gaze flicked to the rings. 'You're returning your rings. I've driven you away. Because you can never love me as much as I love you.'

Her jaw dropped, joy breaking the dam of her terror. 'You *love* me? But—'

'I had a deplorable way of showing it? I'm aware of that. I made false assertions at every opportunity. I neglected you and barely listened to you because I knew I wasn't worthy. I feared you would come to your senses one day and call my bluff on all of it.'

'So you're saying my gamble paid off? That coming to New York actually worked?' she dared to tease.

His nostrils flared. 'Watching you step out of that lift was both heaven and hell. I'd missed you, but I was terrified you were there to tell me that would be the last time I saw you.' His hand dropped to her belly, reverentially caressing it. 'That I would be a father from afar when it was the last thing I wanted.'

Her eyes brimmed with happy tears. 'You love me, Caye? Truly?'

Firm hands cradled her jaw, his eyes gleaming with the depth of feeling. 'So much. I was so desperate, I dumped donations anonymously into your charity in the hope that it would keep you too busy to leave me.'

Her eyes flare wide. 'That was you?'

'I'm not quite ready to divulge all my sins, but know that I've been watching, and am extremely proud of every achievement. And I will continue to support you any way you'll let me.'

'I love you. I love you so much, Cayetano. I was desperate I was losing you too. I'm so happy I'm not.'

She lunged forward and he caught her in his arms, his eager lips finding hers in relief, in love, in desperate reunion.

Mareka wasn't sure how long they stay locked together until a throat cleared delicately.

Ms Smythe watched them from across the room. 'Will I still be valuing the rings?' she asked.

'Only if it's so she can choose another one,' Caye responded before she could speak, because apparently this arrogant love of her life couldn't be cowed for long.

Suppressing a smile, Mareka reached for the rings. 'No, I want to keep them. They'll remind me what I've fought for. That it's been worth it.'

Cayetano sucked in a breath, his eyes darkening. 'Say that again.'

'It's been worth it, to know, to feel, that you love me.'

He took the rings and slid them one by one onto her

finger. 'I vow this to you, *agapita*—you will never have cause to question my love ever again.'

'And I promise that, wherever you are, my heart will be the home you can come to for ever. Now, take me home. Let's start our lives properly.'

He swung her into his arms, his breath-taking smile lighting every corner of her world. 'What are you doing?'

'This was how it started. It is right that this is how it should continue. Besides, you have the rest of your collection to try on.'

'My collection?'

He nodded. 'The one that goes with the bracelet I had Ariana slip into your things two weeks ago.'

'Oh, my God, no wonder I didn't recognise it.'

'I needed my hope to reside next to your skin. I was thrilled when she told me how much you love it.'

He kissed her again as they stepped into the room that held her new, personal collection. The room where Mareka had sat all those months ago and picked the diamond that had led her into love. And, as she sat down, the lightest fluttering in her belly made her gasp.

Cayetano stilled. 'What is it?'

'I think our little one agrees. I just felt the tiniest, sweetest movement.'

Eyes filled with wonder and love, he lowered his head and kissed her. 'I love you. And I love our little one. With everything I am.'

'And we love you back. A million times over.'

EPILOGUE

Ten months later

'WILL THIS COLLECTION ever be complete?' Mareka tried for exasperation, but her heart was too full, the soft sleeping bundle in her arms making her joy overflow.

The enigmatic Ms Smythe had disappeared once more, as she always did after laying out her magnificent creations, leaving the Figueroa family alone.

'I can't help it when every piece looks so exquisite on the mother of my child.'

'Just the mother of your child?' she teased.

Cayetano's eyes flared with love and devotion so pure, she gasped. And, when he reached out and caressed their son Javier's cheek, her heart tumbled over.

'Choose your diamonds, my love. Then allow me to take you home so I can have the honour of showing you just how much I love and treasure you.'

* * * * *